Black Mountain Monsters

Tales From The Black Mountain Triangle

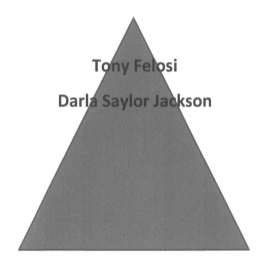

Tony Felosi

Darla Saylor Jackson

Cover Design Zac Caudill

Cover Photography Paul Browning

Introduction

Black Mountain in Harlan County, with an elevation of 4,145 feet, is the tallest peak in the state of Kentucky. It is the crown jewel of the southeastern Kentucky mountain range and contains a vast amount of folklore, legends, and strange occurrences. Most think the name refers to the rich seams of coal located on and around it, but "Black Mountain" is also said to have gotten its name from the dark and bloody incidents that have happened over time. Oral history suggests that the name was given to the mountain by the Native Americans, who were in awe of the massive black shadow it cast over the land. Its seclusion appears to hold many a sinister secret. From that, tales of creatures and monsters revealing themselves to unsuspecting bystanders have been handed down through the years, with occurrences still happening today.

Highway 160, which crosses Black Mountain from Harlan County into Wise County, Virginia, is a lonesome stretch of road, absent of homes or structures, winding up to the summit and then slowly back down again. It gives travelers a feeling of complete isolation; some claim it is as if you enter another world – a beautiful land of enchantment sometimes interrupted by sheer terror. For it is in those moments that many have encountered sights and beings unknown to the natural world.

The following is a compilation of true accounts in and around the area of Black Mountain and the Black Mountain Triangle. This area stretches from West Virginia, East Tennessee to Somerset, Kentucky. In this triangle, an inexplicable number of disappearances, paranormal activity, UFO and cryptid sightings, and bizarre tales abound. The Black Mountain Triangle has an array of fascinating and mysterious events that have occurred through the years in the Appalachian Mountains, one of the oldest mountain ranges in the world, with the Mammoth Cave system, the world's largest, running underneath.

The Black Mountain Triangle

The Black Mountain Triangle is a land mass with far more of its share of unexplained phenomena, disappearances, and tragedy than it should. Deep in mystery, this area extends from the Pikeville/West Virginia area to the Clinton, Tennessee vicinity and then forms the final point of the triangle in Somerset, Kentucky. Much of this region's history is undocumented, and many records are nonexistent, which only heightens the mystique of the land. The many tales and lore result from oral history being passed down through the years.

The Black Mountain Triangle is home to the two tallest peaks in Kentucky: Big Black Mountain and Pine Mountain. Underground is a portion of the Mammoth Cave system, the largest in the world. Harlan County, in its entirety, is within the triangle, with Bell, Leslie, Knox, Whitley, Perry, Laurel, Wayne, Clay, and Pike Counties also contributing to the area. The Cumberland Gap and Cumberland Falls are notable landmarks within the Black Mountain Triangle.

The Triangle has every form of paranormal event one can think of. Cyptid encounters, UFO sightings, ghosts, shadow people, and many other strange phenomena are abundant. There are sightings of strange humans, tiny people, phantom lights, and many more obscure activities within this land mass.

Disappearances and unsolved murders are also plentiful within the Black Mountain Triangle. This could be due to the isolated, unpopulated areas, but it has more than much larger forested and mountainous regions. Disappearances go back to the Civil War era and continue to the present. Many farmers tending their cattle never returned home. Many officials searching for moonshine stills never made it out of the mountains. Although there are logical explanations for these, some defy logic.

In Cumberland, a young boy by the name of Miller went out to get firewood one night and was never seen again. His tracks led out to the woodpile and then stopped. The young man seemed to have vanished within minutes with no other footprints in the snow. Many others seem to have been scooped up by unseen hands with no evidence leading to an explanation.

Many tragedies occur in the Triangle, from murder to plane crashes. There are many solved and unsolved murders, with several victims unidentified. The area holds tight to its secrets and rarely gives them up. Plane crashes can be explained by the tall mountains and fog within the Black Mountain, but what about the ones that crash on clear days in valleys and near roadways?

The feuds and bloodshed within the Triangle are nearly endless. The violence that has erupted in the area is unimaginable, from family fights to the coal wars. The Civil War added to the conflicts, as well as the moonshining era. Even today, sadly, violence is commonplace in the Black Mountain Triangle.

We may never know why this stretch of land is so tumultuous, but it is a vast wealth of material and research for those interested in mystery and the unknown. An infinite supply of secrets is yet to be solved, and the unexplained waiting to be understood.

Welcome to the Black Mountain Triangle.

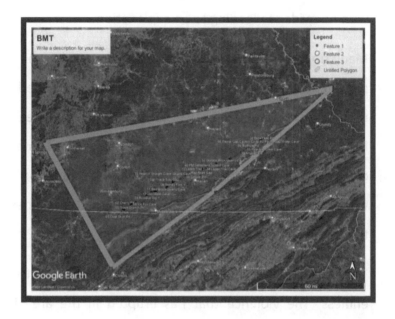

The area known as the Black Mountain Triangle.

The Curse of Black Mountain

The Black Heart Book, the Hardship, and the Healing

This is a comprehensive look at David Alex Turner, the unleashing of a curse, and the tragedy and hardship that ensued for over 100 years. It details the attempt to heal a land ravaged by mineral extraction and those who fell victim to companies exploiting them.

The book, "The Black Heart Book," by David Alex Turner's great-granddaughter, Rosezelle Boggs Qualls, tells the true story of how her great-grandfather unleashed a curse upon the land under the instruction of a mysterious book that came to Harlan County by way of Pittsburgh, Pennsylvania. The following is a look at this incredible tale and how it may have forever changed the area's history.

Until 1898, Big Black Mountain could be best described as a volcano of energy just waiting to erupt. Some have portrayed the mountain as having unseen gates bursting at the hinges, just waiting to be locked. Others have described invisible doors to a portal that only required a key to unlock dark forces bubbling underneath the earth's surface.

David Alex Turner found that key, although he didn't realize it then. The summer of 1898 was a tumultuous time in his life. Born in 1822, he was in his 70s, and the thing he held dear – his property – was under question. He was proud of acquiring a large amount of acreage, and now a neighbor was disputing his ownership in a court of law. No doubt, this made him feel a loss of control and power. These feelings sparked the following events that would change his life and possibly the lives of future generations.

It was only a few weeks after the trial that a traveling salesman came to the small community at the headwaters of Little Greasy Creek, which is now the Big Laurel/Bledsoe, Kentucky area that is across Pine Mountain from what is now Cumberland, Kentucky. In the late 1800s, Cumberland was called "Poor Fork," and Harlan was called "Mount Pleasant."

The salesman had traveled from Poor Fork across the Little Shepherd Trail and to the homeplace of Mr. Turner, where he always made lucrative sales. The Turner family and their neighbors had few opportunities to shop or have new items available to them. The salesman who came from Pennsylvania via Virginia was always a welcome sight. David allowed him to stay the night, and as a "thank you," he gave David Alex Turner an older edition of a Pittsburgh newspaper, another welcome treat. The very educated Mr. Turner could not get enough current reading material; after the salesman departed, he began reading voraciously.

David enjoyed the advertisements nearly as much as the headlines. While going over each item for sale, one in particular caught his attention:

"For sale, take control of your life. Learn the secrets of life and the almighty.

Write Ad #1303, care of this Newspaper. Send two dollars in Postal Stamps.

The book will be sent immediately by return mail."

- *The Black Heart Book, Qualls, page 13*

These events alone could be interpreted as unusual. Who was the salesman? It is insinuated that David Turner knew him and periodically came to the area. The fact that the specific newspaper had the cryptic ad is also very coincidental. It all seemed to be a well-devised plan to attract a man who needed to feel he had regained control of his life. Most people assume this is all circumstantial, but one must admit, it's all very curious. An additional point of interest is the word "almighty." This word, which is generally capitalized, was not. When we refer to the Lord in its many variations, it is always capitalized out of respect and reverence. Also, the ad was number 1303, highlighting number 13, considered unlucky to those superstitious and having particular importance in the "dark arts." This is in Quall's book on page 13, which is also noteworthy.

The advertisement immediately intrigued David, and he gathered his postage, which was the same as currency back then. He got his envelope ready, and he and his daughter, Judy, traveled over Pine Mountain to Putney, where the nearest post office was. He mailed the order and waited impatiently.

It was nearly six weeks before David returned to Putney. There, he learned that his package had arrived the day before. He quickly grabbed the parcel wrapped in dark, coarse paper tied by twine. It was dated September 19, 1898, with no return address. David quickly found a counter and tore into the paper. He discovered a jet-black book of what was described as "combed cowhide," which is cow leather with a little of the fur still intact.

The book's title was written in bright red calligraphy and appeared handwritten. It had gold leaf-edged paper and seemed to be an original work. There were no signs of it being mass-produced. The title read:

Black Heart Book –

Instructions for Understanding Life

Mr. Turner found no copyright page, printing house name, or table of contents as he examined his new treasure. Being educated and well-read, it was obvious to him that this book was a handmade, original creation.

This only added to the mystique; he was more eager than ever to get home and read his book.

He and Judy made their way over Little Shepherd Trail and made it safe and sound despite being stalked by a panther. David went immediately to his room and began delving into his book. He immediately noticed that the beautiful vines framing the handwritten text were snakes upon close examination.

The Black Heart Book discussed leaders, both successful and otherwise. It explained the reason for both and claimed the successes were because they held the power of the Black Heart Book. The third chapter gave an outline of power that could be obtained, and then, to David's excitement, clear, concise instructions were listed.

Wait for the full moon. Climb the highest promontory.

Take no other soul with you. When you reach the top,

wait until midnight. At midnight, shoot three times.

You will receive a sign. Wait in that place. You will receive

further instructions.

Once again, the number "three" shows up in the book. Apprehensive and elated, David Alex Turner is concerned about "cursing the Lord." The highest peak in the area is, of course, Big Black Mountain. He begins pondering this perilous night trek he would have to make. He would have to climb the two tallest mountains in Kentucky, Pine Mountain and Big Black. Although hesitant about this wicked and risky journey, he gets the almanac and finds that the next full moon is Saturday, October 29th.

Although indecisive about the ritual, he continues reading. The Black Heart Book talks about charming animals, healing disease, and changing someone's character for your benefit. During the following days, David showed no one the book and battled with himself regarding the decision to do the ritual and gain power.

Chapter six gave the incantation of the words that should be said during the ritual on top of Big Black Mountain. October 28th found him restless and unable to sleep, and on October 29th in the afternoon, Mr. Turner began his long excursion to the top of Big Black Mountain. He must first travel over Pine Mountain, go through the town of Poor Fork, through the area that is now the cities of Benham and Lynch, and then the grueling trip up the side of the mountain.

He makes it before midnight and is on what is described as a plateau. The moon was bright and illuminated the meadow he was standing in. At midnight, he does just as the Black Heart Book instructed. He shot three times in the air and then chanted, "I curse you, God," three times aloud. Upon saying this, what felt like a bolt of lightning traveled through his body. Then, a silver three-legged bowl dropped out of nowhere and contained three blood drops. To his amazement, the three drops of blood form thin lines connecting each other into what is assumed to be a triangle. The bowl became "white hot," and David quickly dropped it.

Now terrified, David Alex Turner wants nothing more than to retreat from the mountain and act as if this has never happened. Regret and fear are his dominant emotions as he quickly descends the mountain. Within minutes, he is encountered by a huge black dog with a silver studded collar and eyes that look like "red hot embers." Its salivating tongue was between two huge fangs as it spoke in a low growl.

"Alex, go back. Alex, there is more. Alex, I command you to go back." – Qualls, page 20.

Mr. Turner responded, "No," but had no choice but to retreat up the mountain. He waited about 20 minutes before attempting to leave, and to his relief, the dog was gone. He made the rough, exhausting trip home, arriving around 5 AM. In a haze of remorse, David Alex Turner threw the Black Heart Book into the fire and allowed it to burn into ashes. He began praying for forgiveness and desperately sought answers as to how to undo the ritual he had done.

He then decided he must return to Big Black Mountain to reverse the spell he had performed. He traveled once again to the top of the mountain. He found the silver bowl and shot it three times. The bowl struck a rock on the third hit and bounced out of sight. Although Mr. Turner felt he had reversed the spell, the fact that the dog doesn't appear again suggests he just enhanced it by his actions of "threes." Had the dog needed to direct him, it would have surely appeared. Its absence is likely because David Alex Turner did precisely what was required of him.

The rest of the book tells of the rest of the life of Turner. He died in 1929, well over 100 years old, and tried apologetically to follow God for the rest of his life. Although his intentions were selfish and his regret was huge, David Alex Turner may have been a tool to "erupt" the energy of Big Black Mountain – the gates burst open, and the doors opened widely. After ages of dormancy, this act finally released the bubbling dark presence on the mountain.

About 20 years after the ritual performed by David Alex Turner, big industry came to the town of Poor Fork, now Cumberland, Kentucky. Two new cities were built for the purpose of coal – Benham and Lynch, and it seemed to be a miraculous event for Harlan County.

This area is now called the "Tri-City" area, with three towns forming the community. International Harvester, headed up by industrialist Andrew Carnegie, was from Pittsburgh, Pennsylvania, where the Black Heart Book supposedly originated. Drastic changes ensued over the following years, and the lay of the land no longer resembled the sleepy Appalachian town it once was. There were theaters, professional ball teams, a massive hotel, and people from all walks of life speaking many different languages resided there. Some people exited ships at Ellis Island and immediately got on trains headed to Lynch, Kentucky. By today's standards, the equivalence of billions of dollars was spent at the foot of Big Black Mountain before the first ton of coal was ever extracted.

Soon after the kingdom was built, coal as black as the Black Heart Book was mined in world record proportion. From then on, the terms "Black Gold," "Black Diamond," and so on were familiar terms. It was as if the Black Heart Book was coming to life. The extravagantly wealthy industrialists controlled the population just like the book stated. It controlled animals, tools, and the character of men.

The introduction of the coal industry was very prosperous for some. For others, it required uprooting to an unfamiliar location and attempting to be productive with others who didn't speak your language. Although some businessmen made a fortune, there was no money being made by the coal miners. You got paid in the form of "scrip," which was basically "play money" that could be used only at the company store. Most miners worked for food and a place to stay, ultimately enslaved by the coal mine. Very similar to the enslaved people who were forced to construct the pyramids for the Egyptians, the miners seemingly made monuments and landmarks for royalty with no real wage. The laborers died on a regular basis, and even though it was declared "the safest coal mine in the country," the mining industry is a deadly one. Thousands of men lost their lives at a young age.

Suppose one looks at the various symbolism of the newly constructed coal camps. In that case, it is unusual that most of the basic houses have pyramid-shaped roofs, which is a unique architectural feature. The word "portal" isn't commonly used with mines, but is the term used with Portal 30, 31, and 32, which raises the question of why these mines begin at 30? Some have suggested that the supervisors may have belonged to an organization where "level 30" becomes rather dark and mysterious. In contrast, others speculate it is another way to use the number three repetitively without being conspicuous. Obviously, Portal 31 reversed is 13. The definition of a portal is an "imposing entrance."

Later in the 20th century, the coal industry declined. The falling economy couldn't handle the expense of the massive infrastructure, and the communities began falling into ruin. Mountain tops were removed, and the once beautiful mountain ranges were destroyed. Unemployment was high, and morale was low. Drug addiction became a sad reality, and the industry that created us left us to die.

Over the past 100 years, one cannot deny that the area in and around Big Black Mountain has been chaotic and riddled with death, destruction, violence, and crime. The mountain seems to be the crown jewel in an area that is abundant with paranormal activity, now referred to as "The Black Mountain Triangle." Then, there are dog sightings that go back to the early 1900s. These are not typical dogs – they are huge, primarily black or dark, and have a certain human quality, not in appearance as much, but in character. Their eyes seem to know you. As in one story told in this book, they may be shapeshifters going from human to dog form at will. Dogs are not a common paranormal sighting but encounters with these dogs around Big Black Mountain and Harlan County are plentiful. Could the dog encountered by David Alex Turner be the precursor for all the dog sightings in Harlan County? Some think so. This demonic symbol of the curse of the Black Heart Book is still occurring today.

In 2004, Rosezelle Boggs Qualls introduced the world to her family's story in "The Black Heart Book." A few years later, a man named Rick Clendenon, a pastor, was writing a book about the history of his hometown, Lynch, Kentucky. In his research, Rick came across Quall's book and was fascinated. After learning about David Alex Turner performing the ritual and cursing God, Rick Clendenon felt that the curse was still active and needed to cease.

Rick was a much-loved evangelist who frequently returned to his hometown to lead church services. He usually traveled through Virginia and over Black Mountain to get to Lynch. It was on one of these trips that Rick had a vision. He was on top of the mountain and suddenly could see the layers of evil of Big Black Mountain. God told him that specific demons ruled different sections of the mountain. As he traveled down Black Mountain, he was presented with the atrocities layered and embedded into Big Black Mountain. On his descent, he entered the layers of murder, rape, manipulation, greed, theft, deception, and others. He lost all track of time and didn't know how long he had been on the mountain. He was utterly inundated with visions of tragedy and terror. After this trip, he was confident God was calling him to break this curse.

During this time, Rick was also attending a family reunion at Lynch. A young relative, also in attendance, was staying at a place called Solomon's Porch, which is a place where missionaries can stay while working in the area. The young man had been dabbling in black magic and other dark arts. While in the privacy of his room, he began performing a ritual. Suddenly, he felt bound or trapped in his room. An evil presence was holding him captive, and while he could not get out, a transformer outside his window exploded. This frightened the young man to the point that he told Rick what had happened and asked to be saved and baptized. The evil presence that had imprisoned the young man was so strong that it enforced Rick's belief that the land needed to be cleansed of wickedness. His goal was to take the land back and give it to God.

Rick Clendenon said that the waters that flowed off Black Mountain, the highest peak, eventually reached the entire state of Kentucky and began planning a prayer service that involved people from all over the state to heal the land. While overseas on a mission trip, Rick contracted a disease that affected his heart. He was told his time was short, and he was urgent to get the healing service completed. Rick firmly believed that Black Mountain was cursed by the Black Heart Book and the ritual performed by David Alex Turner in 1898.

In the late 2000s, after reading much scripture on the subject, Rick Clendenon organized a religious service to break the curse of the Black Heart Book. He wanted a representative from each county in Kentucky to be in attendance. He said that God gave him a vision of the service at the Lynch Country Club parking lot, which is at the foot of Big Black Mountain. The parking lot was to be used as the base and used for praise and worship with music. Then, he took the representatives and set them out on areas of the mountain at each level of evil, and they were given specific times to pray. People were dropped off all over the mountain to pray simultaneously to rid the mountain of the curse and remove the evil that dwelled there. There is an ancient belief that from the top of your head to the highest peak in the area is where God resides. This is the reason for the prayer service there and maybe why David Alex Turner was instructed to go to the top of Black Mountain in the first place.

After the healing prayer services, Rick's last mission was to create a monument to commemorate the three prayer vigils and the ceremony to take the land back. With help from friends and local ministries, he designed and erected a triangular-shaped monument with biblical specifications. Everything about the monument was well thought out and planned as a lasting reminder that Big Black Mountain was given back to God.

Things have improved after the prayer service. The economy has improved, as well as the mindset of the people. The sense of community is strengthening again, and the Tri-City area is reviving. Rick Clendenen has since passed away, but the reviving community and monument at Lynch reminds us of a man who loved his community so much he battled against evil and fought to rid the land of the Curse of Black Mountain.

The pyramid shaped monument, Lynch, Kentucky.

Men In Black at the FAA Radar Tower

Accounts of Men in Black have been reported since the 1940s. John Keel's 1975 book, The Mothman Prophecies, coined the term "Men In Black," which later was the name of a famous movie in the 1990s. Men In Black supposedly appear to people who have witnessed UFO activity and intimidate them into not discussing or reporting it. They are dressed in black business suits and drive black cars. They do not act like "normal" humans, and it is suspected they are aliens in disguise.

The Federal Aviation Administration built a Long-Range Radar site on Black Mountain to identify and track military and civilian aircraft movements within a 200-mile radius and to provide air-ground radio communication with those aircraft. Nicknamed "The Golf Ball," the tower has been the source of speculation and unusual sightings since its first existence. It is hard to deny that if UFOs do exist, the FAA Radar Tower would probably be very attractive to them. That may explain the unusual amount of UFO sightings in that area.

Besides unidentified flying objects being spotted, many witnesses claim they see other strange activity near the tower. One of these is black SUVs that frequently lurk around the tower. Some people have observed several black SUVs making their way up to the top of Black Mountain. The passengers of the vehicles are very pale, stoic men dressed in what appears to be black suits and ties. Recent sightings of the vehicles suggest they are Chevrolet Tahoes.

Others claim that the radar tower is the location of strange rituals. People claim to see cloaked individuals making their way to the tower or standing at its base, seemingly performing a type of ceremony. Their unusual appearance makes onlookers wary of approaching or inquiring what they are doing. Some hikers claim to see odd symbols carved in trees, rocks, and the ground near the tower.

The FAA Radar Tower is a unique structure in its own right. It is easy to see how it could attract beings of many interests, whether ritualistic or galactic. Although its purpose is widely known, it appears to be a monument and silent watcher of the unusual and unexplained.

FAA Radar on Black Mountain, AKA "The Golf Ball"

David Hartford is a native of Lynch, Kentucky, and this experience happened when he was a 15-year-old student at Lynch High School.

The Ghost of Maria

David was in shop class one day when his friend, Kenny, claimed that his dad had seen a ghost in the old Influenza Cemetery while returning from squirrel hunting. The Influenza Cemetery, or the Spanish Flu Cemetery, as some call it, originated from the Spanish Flu epidemic of 1918 when people were dying rapidly. Kenny's dad was walking home by the cemetery when he saw a mist forming. Through the fog came the ghost of a woman.

Mike, who was also in the class, was interested in the paranormal, and the conversation about the ghost sparked his attention. He quickly approached David and Kenny and suggested they have a séance at the cemetery. He then began to tell them how the flu victims were swiftly buried because of the plague and that they were buried with their valuables. By this time, the whole class began to listen as Mike convinced them that they should dig up the graves and get the jewelry.

Being young and foolish, nine teenage boys decided to attempt to rob the graves of the Spanish Flu Cemetery. They met that evening at 6 o'clock at Lynch High School. David, along with his dog, Kenny, Mike, and the others, set out to the old cemetery at the foot of Black Mountain.

They approached the cemetery, shovels in hand, and began looking around. They saw headstones scattered on the hillside. They came upon a tombstone with the name "Maria" inscribed. The woman had died young, and it appeared one of her children was buried beside her. Mike, the group leader, said they should have a séance and ask Maria permission to dig up her grave.

The boys joined hands, forming a ring around Maria's grave. Mike spoke aloud and asked Maria for permission to dig her up. David had never done anything like this and began feeling very apprehensive about the whole thing. He began to feel a strange energy going from one arm to another. Mike then asked Maria to give them a sign if she didn't want them to dig her up.

Soon after they finished their séance, they heard something roll down the hill. Not thinking anything about it, one boy began digging in the soft dirt of the grave. Suddenly, the shovel hit something and bent, which was very strange because of how soft it had seemed. The boys didn't have time to think about the shovel when one of them began wildly pointing at the hillside.

Among the graves was a young woman wearing a flowing white dress with outstretched arms. She gazed at them expressionless as a mist formed at the hem of her dress. She began walking toward them across a small creek. The boys did not hesitate to take off running, and David even outran his dog, Brisket, who was very fast. They did not stop until they were back at the high school.

The boys, who were looking for an adventure, never dreamed they would actually see a ghost that night. They all learned their lesson and never attempted to harm a grave again.

The grave of Maria at the Spanish Flu Cemetery.

David Hartford and the Black Mountain Monsters

One night several years ago, David Hartford was returning home to Lynch after playing in a softball tournament in Kingsport, Tennessee. As he was coming down the mountain near where the picnic tables used to be, he saw glowing lights. At first, he thought the lights were coon hunters, but he quickly realized they were not. They were three pairs of glowing eyes.

As he approached the lights, David saw three creatures near the road's edge. Two of them darted up where the picnic tables were. The other remained, and as his headlights fell upon it, he saw a massive black dog calmly sitting on the side of the road. It had thick dark fur, and its eyes glowed a soft orange. It had fangs so long that they extended past its chin. The giant beast was at least four feet tall, sitting down, and was much larger had it stood up. David stared in awe at the creature, not believing his eyes. Although not as visible as the dog, he is confident he saw the dark silhouette of a man back in the shadows.

He slowly continued past the dog, who sat very still, never moving an inch. David then looked at the dog through his rearview mirror and could see it even better from this vantage point because of the soft glow of the brake lights. At that point, David felt it was time to go. He sped up and left the creature and the dark figure solemnly sitting by the road.

David has had other encounters since then. In 2018, he and his buddies were going to play golf in South Carolina. They left early, before daybreak, and headed across Black Mountain. They went around a curve near the mountain's peak and saw something sitting in a tree. It was tremendous and hunched over, not moving at all. The closest thing it resembled was a kangaroo with large ears and short fur. It had a long snout, muscular back legs, and short, smaller front legs. Although it did not look like a bird, David and the other men expected it to fly as the car approached. It did not, however, and leaped off the branch and basically off the side of Black Mountain. Nothing could have survived that kind of fall, and the men could never figure out what they saw that early morning. It is possible that the creature jumped off the branch and then flew, but the side of the mountain was straight down at that point, and they never saw it after it leaped.

Another time, David was traveling across Black Mountain one night near the Spanish Flu Cemetery and came upon a creature dragging something across the road. His headlights hit the creature, and he noticed that there were two more creatures, one of them standing upright. David is sure these were not bears or coyotes. Startled and concerned about what was being dragged, David shot at the creature. He is convinced he hit the creature, but the shot didn't affect it whatsoever, and it continued dragging what appeared to be a deer carcass with the other two following it - one on all fours and the other upright and walking like a human. David claims this is one of the most disturbing things he's ever seen.

David has had many experiences on Black Mountain and believes that devil dogs, along with other cryptids yet to be discovered, lurk on that mountain.

The Angel in the Hospital

In 2016, David Hartford had an ingrown toenail that wouldn't heal because he had diabetes. After trying to deal with it at home, he decided to go to the Harlan Appalachian Regional Hospital, where he was quickly admitted. The doctors told him that he had MRSA, and it was severe. The antibiotics weren't working, and he might lose his toe, foot, leg, or even life. The infection was working its way up his leg, and nurses were measuring the speed at which it traveled through his body.

This was very upsetting to David, and he feared for his life. He began praying for God to send an angel and heal his leg. He was sitting in bed terrified and could not sleep. He had surgery scheduled the next morning, and part of his body would surely be amputated.

Sometime after midnight, a man walked into David's hospital room and said, "My son, my son, may I pray for you?" David told him that he desperately needed prayer. The man put his hand on David's leg and began praying. At that time, David started to feel a deep feeling of peace. The man took out a piece of purple cloth, laid it on David's leg, turned, and walked away. David thanked him as he left, and the man turned around and said, "My son, keep faith and keep believing."

The following day, David awakes to one of the doctors walking in his room. He looks at David's foot and exclaims, "Oh my God!" David now fears the worst and is sure he will lose his leg. He asked the doctor how bad it was, and the doctor told him to look for himself. David looks at his foot, and it is completely healed. The infection was gone.

Amazed, the doctor said the antibiotic must have kicked in, and David said no. An angel came last night and healed him. The doctor told David that he believed it, too. Relieved that all that needed to be done was a toenail removal, David took his prayer cloth with him to the procedure.

David is sure that the man who came to him that night in the hospital was an angel and an answered prayer from God. He is confident that his leg and life were saved because he prayed for help.

The Phantom of Pine Mountain

On Thursday, September 8, 2022, a couple was going home to Bledsoe from Harlan at approximately 10 p.m. They were traveling across Pine Mountain on Highway 421 from Baxter to Bledsoe. It was a clear night with the moon and stars shining brightly in the sky.

As they traveled through an area the locals call "the straight" because it is one of the few places where you can pass safely on the mountain, the woman driving noticed something out the passenger side window. It looked like a huge black figure wearing a cape that formed sharp tips at the tail. The tail of the cape flapped wildly at the ends. She said nothing, thinking that perhaps her eyes played tricks on her. As she watched out of the corner of her eye, the figure sped up and left the car behind, finally veering to the right and purposely going over the side of the mountain. Since she was on the stretch of road that allowed her to go faster, she was going at least 55 miles per hour. The figure had to have been going over 80 miles per hour.

As soon as the figure darted over the mountain, her husband, who also saw it, said, "Did you just see that?" Now she knew she wasn't seeing things. She told him she had. Her husband wasn't driving and got a better look at the figure. According to him, it appeared at the beginning of the straight. It stayed right beside the car for the first few seconds. It was around 12 feet tall and seemed like a black figure wearing a cape with pointy tips. The tips were large and flew up in the air as the figure effortlessly glided 55 miles per hour. Then, halfway through the straight, it picked up speed and sprinted ahead of the car, going right over the mountain's edge. Both people in the car saw the exact same thing. There was no denying that something had really been out there.

I was told about the account the next day and was very intrigued, especially since I am originally from Bledsoe. I also know the couple well, and they were undoubtedly telling the truth. I told another friend from Bledsoe about the bizarre occurrence. To my surprise, she had her own tales about the exact figure.

In 2010, Shannon was standing by her microwave oven, and while she waited for her food, she stared out of the kitchen window that faced Highway 421. She saw something white speed by on the wrong side of the road. According to her, it was snow white, had white hair that formed pointed tips, and wore a cape that formed pointy tips at the tail. It was enormous and held its hands as if holding handlebars. It appeared to have a shredded shirt that hung down around its elbows. Although this was a peculiar sight, she returned to fixing dinner and never thought any more about it.

That is, until one morning when she was walking her dog before work. It was just getting daylight, and the fog was thick in the valley. Up the road a bit, about 90 yards away, she spotted what appeared to be the exact figure in the fog. It was standing at the end of a driveway on the side of the road. It looked just like the figure she had seen speeding down the road. She quickly got her dog and went inside her house. When she left for work, the figure was gone.

Shannon hadn't thought much about the white figure in a week or so when her sister, who is also her neighbor, told her that she had seen a white figure going down the road. She wanted to get in her car and follow it, but it was much too fast. Their mother overheard them and told them she had seen the same thing, only it was going up the road.

Their mother is Shannon's other neighbor. The three live side by side. One night, a week or so later, Shannon's sister said she saw a vast white figure sitting on her mother's back porch. It was so big that its head nearly hit the top of her porch even sitting down. Her mother's motion light came on, and nothing was there. Her sister definitely saw something, and something had to set off the light's motion sensor.

A few months later, Shannon's sister was at their mother's house when they witnessed an old man walking up the middle of the road. He had two extremely tall tree branches in each hand, as if he were using them to help him walk. As he slowly made his way down the road, the two women stayed back in the living room and peeked through the blinds so he couldn't see them. He had weathered skin and was very skinny. To their surprise, when he got in front of the house, he turned his head slowly and stared back at them. They jumped away from the window, and the old man was gone when they looked back.

When they told Shannon about it, the one thing that caught her attention was how the old man was holding his arms out with the tall branches. She remembered that was the same way the white figure had been holding his hands, too, only he had nothing in them.

About six months after the 2022 incident, and after we had talked about it, Shannon had returned home from a doctor's appointment and was standing in her living room. She noticed something in the window and saw the tip of a black cape as a dark, translucent figure walking toward the road. She is sure that is what the couple saw on Pine Mountain and thinks the dark figure can turn white at times, depending on the time of day. She also thinks it sometimes appears as an old man.

No one is sure what this phenomenon really is, but Shannon and her family call it "The Phantom." I felt that was a fitting name, so for now, it is called "The Phantom of Pine Mountain." This phantom lurks around Highway 421, from Baxter to Bledsoe and then to Beech Fork in

Leslie County. It will appear at any time of day, so if you are traveling over Pine Mountain, be on the lookout for the Phantom of Pine Mountain.

Pine Mountain, Harlan County, Kentucky

Bigfoot Creature of Little Black Mountain

Black Mountain is a huge mountain range with two prominent peaks: Big Black Mountain, located in the Tri-City area of Harlan County, and Little Black Mountain, located in the Evarts area of the county. These events happened in the Black Mountain community at the base of Little Black Mountain.

Linda and her family have lived in the community of Black Mountain for over 50 years. She and her husband have raised a large family and now have grandchildren and great-grandchildren living nearby.

In July 2010, Linda's granddaughter, Laura, was enjoying the summer break from school. She would go and get her friends, and they would spend the night several times a week. On this particular night, Laura had driven to pick up her two best friends who lived in Evarts. On the ride home, they discussed what movies they would watch and what snacks they would prepare. The neighborhood dogs caught their attention as Laura turned up the little lane to go to her house. Several dogs were facing toward Laura's house and were barking ferociously.

Because she was driving, Laura had to look back at the road. When she did, she noticed a monstrous creature standing in the middle of a small, paved driveway. It was dark brown, and its eyes glowed red in the beam of the headlights. It only stood there a second before it leaped over the hill in one giant stride. As the other girls in the girl turned back to face the road, the creature was gone. That was indeed what the dogs had been barking at.

The girls quickly ran into the house in fear the beast would return. Laura called her grandmother, Linda, and told her all about it. The next day, she showed her an overhanging limb where the creature stood, nearly hitting its head on it. By that estimation, it would have been over eight feet tall. Linda asked if it could have possibly been a bear, and Laura adamantly stated that she got a perfect look at it and there was no way it could have been a black bear.

Linda lives next door to her daughter's house, where Laura lives, and saw the massive beast at the top of her driveway. Several years after Laura's sighting, Linda was home cleaning the house. As she did so, she began washing dishes and looking out the window above the sink. She noticed that beside a small stream coming down from the mountain, she saw what appeared to be a "gorilla" looking creature squatting down by the stream's edge. It seemed to have a large domed head and was silvery black. Certain she was creating this with her mind, she went on about her housework. A few minutes later, she returned to the kitchen and looked out the window again. It still looked like a huge animal was squatted down by the stream. She stared at it some more, and this time, it seemed to have moved its arm somewhat, like it was swatting a fly.

Refusing to believe what she saw, she again attributed it to a trick of the eye and possibly a swift breeze blowing a limb to and fro. She headed down the hall to finish up, and about an hour later, she returned to the kitchen and, of course, looked out the window. This time, she was shocked to see that the creature was gone. It no longer looked like something was squatting by the stream. It looked like it always did. It was then that Linda was convinced that there had, indeed, been a large creature sitting by the little mountain stream behind her house.

From then on, Linda is sure of what she saw and is convinced that Laura saw something similar that warm summer night in July. She and her family know something else resides in their little family neighborhood at the foot of Little Black Mountain.

Bizarre Sights and Sounds at Cranks Lake

Cranks Lake is sometimes referred to as "The Old Lake." It was there prior to the larger Martins Fork Lake, and both lakes are within a mile or two of one another. An unusual feature of Cranks Lake is that you can't access the lakeshore by walking entirely around it. One side of the lakeshore is at Cranks, while the other side is at Smith. You can see the Smith side and vice versa, but it's about a 15- or 20-minute drive from each other.

Michelle Carroll Cole is a native of Cranks, Kentucky, and spent much of her childhood at Cranks Lake. She and her husband, Randy, still frequently camp, hike, and fish on the Cranks and Smith sides of the lake. In the fall of 2017, Michelle and Randy decided to camp at a place on the Cranks side called Troublesome. Troublesome is a road that ultimately dead ends at the lakeshore, as do all roads leading to that area. They picked a spot where the road crossed a creek to spend the night to set up their hammocks and sleep.

They had both fallen asleep when a strange sound suddenly awakened them. It was a low-moaning howl. Michelle is very familiar with all the animals in the area, and this was not a coyote, fox, or bear. They listened to the sound, and luckily, it didn't move or get closer. It seemed to stay in one place. They did not leave and finally went back to sleep after the howling subsided, but Michelle claimed that the howls were somewhat scary and nothing she had ever heard before.

In the same place a few months later, in the spring of 2018, Michelle, Randy, and their dog, Biscuit, were hiking at Troublesome. Michelle noticed that everything had become eerily silent and strange when Biscuit, a gentle, friendly dog, suddenly stopped dead in his tracks and wouldn't move anymore. He would look ahead and growl but would not go any further. Biscuit is a Great Pyrenees Lab mix, so he couldn't be forced to continue the walk. However, he eagerly walked back to the truck from where they had come from. Michelle isn't certain what scared Biscuit that day, but she also felt a strange presence or feeling.

Monkeys in the Mountains

In the mountains of Harlan County, there seem to be sightings and encounters of animals that are not supposed to be there. These are creatures not native to the area and supposedly cannot survive in the terrain and climate. Panthers and other varieties of exotic cats are the prime example. For nearly 100 years, there have been claims of witnessing large cats in Harlan County and surrounding areas that cannot possibly be our Kentucky Wildcat, also known as the Bobcat. My grandfather had his own tales of panthers trying to get his family's chickens in the 1920's. As a young boy in Leslie County, he often told me about looking outside in the middle of the night and seeing giant panthers stalking the chicken coup. He described them as one would a black panther or even a leopard. Photographs of exotic cats in the Appalachian Mountains frequently turn up, some authentic, others not.

The Department of Fish and Wildlife vehemently denies these cats' existence, saying that the environment and animal population could not sustain animals of that size and appetite. Meanwhile, those who have encountered these beasts insist that southeastern Kentucky, southwest Virginia, and West Virginia are home to "jungle cats." There have been theories about how these creatures came to call our mountains home. One legend tells of a circus or carnival caravan traveling through the Cumberland Gap when one of the horse-pulled wagons got stuck. While getting the wagon back on the road, the exotic animals it was hauling escaped into the forest, never to be recaptured. If this is true, the cats seen today may be the descendants or hybrids of these jungle cats. Another more recent explanation is a story out of West Virginia that claims an owner of an exotic petting zoo died, and his family didn't know what to do with the animals, so they freed them into the wild. A released lion ate much of the cattle and livestock in the area before it was captured and sent to a big cat sanctuary in Indiana.

Wolves are another species of animals frequently spotted in Harlan County and not supposed to be there. Although once native to Kentucky, the wolf population was eradicated in the 1800s. However, many Harlan

County residents say they see grey wolves and are sure they are not coyotes. There have been recent sightings in the Evarts area of the county and as current as 2019 in the community of Benham. A couple traveling from Benham to Lynch claim to have seen a large grey wolf right outside of Benham and that it was in no way a coyote. This was mid-day, and they both got a good look at the animal. The large canines can most certainly survive in the climate and once thrived in Kentucky until human contact. Some explain them away by saying they are giant coyotes or dog/wolf mixes that were once pets. Either way, wolf sightings in southeastern Kentucky are common.

The most unique creature said to live in Harlan County, which is not native to Kentucky, is the monkey. Small primates have been seen for at least 60 years, maybe longer. In 1976, a woman from Benham, Kentucky, claimed that monkeys were living in an area nearby called "Machine Shop Hollow." There are many reasons why monkeys should not be in the Appalachian Mountains. Monkeys are not native to the United States. Although they once called North America home, climate change made it impossible for them to survive. Florida now has a population of non-native monkeys in the Ocala area due to a Tarzan movie filmed at Silver Springs in 1939 that did not collect their monkey extras after filming. It has also been suggested that monkeys were released in Florida in the 1930s to increase tourism. These monkeys thrive in the warm Florida climate and are now considered pesky neighbors who get into mischief and do not mind their own business. They steal food and harass pets, according to Ocala area residents.

Monkeys living in Florida isn't a far stretch, but monkeys in Harlan County are somewhat unbelievable. However, the reports of monkey sightings continue to grow. In the book Haunted Harlan County, we told of a 1968 experience that involved someone bringing a dead monkey out of the woods at Lynch, at the foot of Black Mountain. This primate was around 3 to 4 feet tall and was covered with fur. After it was shown around the community, it was tossed out in the woods again.

In the 1970s, miners on their way home from work witnessed a monkey in the snow at Cloverlick. They were so amazed that the driver nearly wrecked. Later, another man driving down Black Mountain into Lynch claimed to see a monkey on the side of the road. The monkeys spotted on the roadsides were relatively small and had long tails. The larger one found dead seemed different and more apelike.

Although it seems impossible for these tropical animals to survive the winters of Kentucky, accounts of seeing monkeys in Harlan County are relatively plentiful. Edmond Gross says he was also told of monkeys in Harlan County, these being in the Martins Fork area.

In 1980, Edmond and his friend went squirrel hunting at Cranks Lake near the dam at a place called Bear Pen. Edmond drove his hunting buddy to the mouth of a hollow, let him out, and was going to park his truck near the road. He had just exited his vehicle and began walking to some hickory trees where he wanted to hunt when his friend came walking down the road toward the truck. Confused, Edmond asked him why he was finished so soon. His friend told him that he wouldn't tell him because he'd laugh at him. Edmond assured him he wouldn't, and the man told him that he had just settled under some hickory trees when he heard the tree branches shaking violently. He looked up to see a monkey swinging from branch to branch. This primate, about three or four feet tall, was the size of a six-year-old child. It stood on a large branch and curiously peered down at him. It then went back in the direction it came from. Edmond's friend didn't wait to see what the monkey would do next. He headed out of the hollow and back to the truck. That ended the hunting trip for that day.

It is hard to say what people are seeing in the mountains of Harlan County, but there are definitely creatures out there that break all the rules of nature. Many credible eyewitnesses support the idea that we do not know everything that roams the hills and hollers.

Monkey Creatures of Black Mountain

In the summer of 1968, Bo's father and his buddy came home with a unique discovery. Apparently, they had been at a place called "Football Field Hollow" at Lynch, Kentucky, named this because it is directly behind the Lynch High School football field that is at the base of Black Mountain.

Bo's dad pulled in, lowered the tailgate of his truck, and told Bo, who was six years old then, and the other neighborhood children to come and see what they had found.

Bo recalls seeing an animal lying in the bed of the pickup truck. It appeared to be a monkey about the same size as he was. There was a nylon miner's rope around its neck, and his dad got the rope, pulled the monkey out of the truck, and then hung it up in the coal shed. A coal shed is a small outbuilding, approximately 3x8, used to store coal for fuel and was a standard feature among all the houses at Gap Branch. According to the two men, they had found the monkey dead in the hollow.

The monkey had large eyes, and part of its shin had some bone exposed. It appeared to have been dead for a couple of days. Bo distinctly recalls the small creature with large, flat feet and no thumbs. After they showed the kids, the men put the monkey creature back in the truck and headed down the road to show their buddies.

One of their buddies told them they could get in trouble for having the dead monkey and might even be charged with murder. It seems their buddy considered this creature more human than animal. With that, they took the animal and threw it over a bank going up Black Mountain.

It is unknown what the monkey-like creature really was. Most everyone thought it was a monkey, but at least one person thought it could be at least part human. Speculating, it is possible it could have been a juvenile Bigfoot creature.

There have been other monkey-like creatures spotted in the Lynch area. These creatures do not fit the description of a Bigfoot creature and are smaller, appearing to be more of a small monkey species. Not long ago, a man Bo used to work with was coming down

Black Mountain at Lynch, where the "Kingdom Come State Park 10 Miles" sign is. According to this man, a monkey ran out in the road, came off the mountain, crossed the road in front of him, and continued down the mountain. He said it was a small monkey with a long tail.

In the 1970s, at Cloverlick, Kentucky, near the Lynch sighting, some coal miners were traveling home from work in a large snow when they saw a monkey that nearly caused them to wreck. They, too, say that a monkey came running off the hill, and they were so busy looking at it that they almost ran out of the road. As in the recent sighting, this was a small monkey with a long tail.

An average monkey can't live in the climate of southeastern Kentucky, so these creatures are a mystery. However, a handful of sightings by credible witnesses say monkey-like creatures roam the Black Mountain region.

The following is contributed by the co-author of this book, Tony Felosi.

Norris Lake Bigfoot

In 1985, Tony and his father, Ralph Felosi, camped out at the Chuck Swan State Forest in Sharps Chapel, Tennessee, and on Norris Lake. Ralph and Tony went to Greasy Hollow, several miles from Blue Springs Boat Dock, where they kept their boats.

They set up their camp and turtle lines with a hook connected to stakes in the ground. As they were setting up camp, strange things immediately began happening. Their pontoon began rocking without any nearby boats or strong wind.

Later that night, they began hearing loud growls. They could hear trees being shaken fiercely far back in the forest with large limbs being snapped from them. Just beyond the campfire light, they could hear something walking around. It sounded like large rocks were also being thrown back into the forest. This happened for about an hour and then abruptly stopped. Although bears were not common in that area at the time, and it wasn't typical behavior for them, that was the best excuse they could find for the odd happenings.

The following day, they tried to find evidence but didn't find anything. The second night, right at dusk, the same thing happened as the night before, but this time, it was more violent. It only happened for about half an hour, so they went to their tent and slept. At about 1 a.m., nearby trees started shaking, and just about 10 feet from the tent came a guttural growl, and heavy footsteps pounded the earth. The growl was so loud that Tony could feel it in his chest. This terror went on for a couple of minutes and abruptly stopped again.

As soon as it was daylight, they packed up quickly and left. They felt the safest thing to do was leave because they were obviously in something's territory.

As Tony researched cryptozoology through the years, he learned that what he and his father heard during that camping trip was classic Bigfoot behavior. Although he can't prove it, he now believes he heard an undocumented creature that night.

Tony is not the first of his family to have unusual experiences in that area of Norris Lake. Ralph Felosi, Tony's grandfather, Joe Felosi, and Chuck Hensley were fishing close to the bank in a cabin cruiser, a large fishing boat with accommodations to stay in below deck. Chuck decided to go into the boat and go to bed, but Ralph and Joe decided to stay out and fish longer. They heard someone walking on top of the cruiser in the middle of the night. They both assumed it was Chuck getting back up to fish some more. A few minutes later, Chuck comes out of the boat and asks why they are walking on top of the boat. They told him they had been fishing the entire time.

On other occasions in the 1970s and early 80s, Tony's grandfather would night fish at one of his favorite spots, the led mines. The bank consisted of massive cliffs around 200 to 300 feet high. It would be impossible for someone to access this area by land. He claimed that sometimes he could hear loud growls high up on the cliffs at night. Then, something would throw rocks at his pontoon as if trying to get him to leave. Sometimes, he would leave, but other times he would stay. The stones never hit the float, only around it. Occurrences like this happened in several places around the Blue Springs Boat Dock.

These stories and events around Norris Lake were Tony's first introduction to the possibility of Bigfoot creatures existing and dwelling in the southeastern United States. He is still unsure what he and his family were hearing, but nothing can be explained by any wildlife known in the area.

The Bigfoot Creature of Slope Hollow

In 1983, Bo worked at Karst-Robbins Coal Company near Louellen, Kentucky. Louellen is a coal community located in the Evarts area of Harlan County. Bo and his brother-in-law worked at the coal company and lived in the Tri-Cities area of the county. The men rode to work together and typically left their homes at about 2:30 AM every morning. Because it was the closest route to work, they traveled on a rough road called Slope Hollow. Slope Hollow goes across Black Mountain from Cumberland to the Evarts area and cuts down quite a bit of mileage despite being curvy and bumpy. In 1983, this road was much more challenging to travel than today because it had yet to be paved and was a gravel logging road.

This particular February morning began no differently than any other. Bo picked up his brother-in-law and started their rough trek across Slope Hollow. At about 3 a.m., they had just crossed over the trip's highest point and were going back down on the Louellen side of the mountain. They were about halfway down the mountain and were approaching a significant curve where the creek flows under the road. It is a beautiful spot with a waterfall and large boulders, and Bo was traveling very slow at this point because the road gets exceptionally rocky in this area.

As Bo approached the sharp curve, he could see that on the other side was a prominent figure standing beside the road. This got his attention, and even when he rounded the curve, he kept watching and noticed that it was moving. As he came out of the curve, his headlights hit directly on this figure.

He was about 40 feet from it now and could see this giant creature squatting down on all fours. Bo came to a complete stop and watched the figure stand straight up using perfect posture. It glanced at the jeep and stood in the center of the road with one giant step. Bo and his brother-in-law had an excellent view of the creature and stared straight at it. They could see every detail of this massive being with the headlights on bright.

It stood about 8 feet tall and was facing the creek on the side of the road. Bo stared intently at this creature, trying to process exactly what it was. Neither of the men said a word as they watched this colossal creature. Its head seemed smaller than the rest of its body and had a very short neck. It had huge, broad shoulders that made its head appear even smaller. It slowly turned toward them, stared back at the men for a second, and then turned around to face the creek. Its face can only be described as "that of a monkey."

Bo continued to assess the creature. It had unusually long, lanky arms and was not very muscular in the upper portion of its body. Its upper body was covered with long, shaggy red hair. Its lower body, however, was extraordinarily muscular and toned with a perfect physique that could have been "carved out of stone." Its legs and lower body had much shorter hair, so the definition of the muscles was very noticeable.

It squatted down in a marksman squat position, looked at the men once again, and pounced over into the creek with one jump of its huge muscular legs. Without thinking, Bo jumped out of the jeep to see where it was going. He could hear the mighty creature bounding up the mountain via the creek and was soon gone. As he stood there, he noticed some garbage someone had thrown out and assumed the creature had been going through it looking for food.

Bo got back in the car and asked his brother-in-law if he had just seen all that. He replied that he had. Stunned, they said very little on the rest of the way to work and, in fact, have yet to speak about this incident.

Interestingly, one of Bo's friends claimed to have had a similar experience a couple of weeks later a mile above where Bo's sighting was. This man was near the top of the mountain when a large creature ran down the mountain, crossed in front of his vehicle, jumped into the creek, jumped back out, and ran in front of the jeep a second time. He says this creature was going so fast that its fur flowed in the breeze. This seems to be the same creature that Bo and his brother-in-law encountered.

Bo is certain he saw a Bigfoot creature that cold night in Slope Hollow. Until then, he did not believe in Bigfoot and admits that he still has difficulty believing such a creature exists. Over the past 40 years, he has spent much time in the mountains of Southeast Kentucky and

Southwest Virginia and has never seen anything like the massive, impressive creature he encountered in 1983.

Karst-Robbins Coal Company, Louellen, Kentucky

Supposed Extinct Creatures of Appalachia

If there is one place in the United States where animals presumed to be extinct could still thrive, it is probably the Appalachian Mountains, the oldest mountain range in North America. The Blue Ridge Mountains, part of the Appalachian Range, are 1.2 billion years old. These mountains were nearly as old as time and were home to prehistoric animals throughout the millennia. Some claim that these thought-to-be-extinct animals still roam the hills, cliffs, and hollows of Harlan County. This isn't out of the realm of possibility. Much of the region is a vast forest where humans rarely tread. Another geographic feature that could enable their survival undetected is the cave system that runs throughout the area and is part of the mammoth cave system, the largest in the world. It is possible that prehistoric creatures still live in seclusion within the caves running the span of Harlan County, only coming out when in search of food, warmth, or occasional daylight.

To further strengthen the theory that some animals thought extinct still live in southeastern Kentucky, people have come forward with credible accounts of encountering creatures that do not fit the description of any present-day animals. In our book, Haunted Harlan County, we recounted the experience of McKensi Johnson Gilliam and her father. In July 2010, they were shooting fireworks in their yard at Hiram, Kentucky. A massive creature the size of a car came out of the woods and walked between them all at once. Its legs were as big around as a human, and its feet made a thunderous sound as it lumbered past them. The unusual creature returned to the woods, and they didn't see it again. Years later, they were telling a family member about the beast, and he claimed that he, too, saw it around the same time in Cloverfork, just a few miles from Hiram. The witnesses claimed the creature had no ears or neck, eliminating a black bear common to the area. The fact that it walked on all fours eliminated a bigfoot creature. I was somewhat bewildered about what they saw until I began researching prehistoric animals. The animal that the Johnson family described seems very similar to a giant sloth. The giant ground sloth, also called the Megalonyx, inhabited North America until 9,500 years ago, relatively recent in the scheme of time. It is thought that climate change and Paleoindians aided in their extinction. The mountains and caves of Harlan County could have served as a refuge protecting them from both culprits.

Another remarkable account of encountering a prehistoric creature in modern times is one told by Edmond Gross. An avid outdoorsman all his life, Edmond knows all the creatures of Harlan County well, but in 1979, he saw something he'd never seen before or since. He and his brother were squirrel hunting in the Martins Fork area of the county between Cranks Lake and Martins Fork Lake, sometimes referred to as "the old lake and the new lake." There is a hollow near Cranks Lake called "Bear Pen Hollow," where the two hunters were on this particular day. Edmond's brother was down on the road, while Edmond was at a hickory tree where he had good luck on previous hunting trips.

He was sitting quietly when he heard a loud flapping noise that sounded somewhat like the steam engine of a train. At about that same time, a vast dark mass blocked the sun, casting a shadow over Edmond. This caused him to look up immediately, and when he did, he saw a bird flying overhead with a wingspan of around 16 feet. The flying creature's body was about the size of a small car and had an unusually long neck. As he stared in disbelief, the gigantic birdlike creature moved its head from side to side as if scanning the ground below. It never sailed but continuously flapped its massive wings the entire time as if it were too large to glide as birds usually do. It flew on out of sight, and Edmond never saw it again.

Amazed at what he'd seen, Edmond tried to identify what kind of bird it was. He went to the library, and nothing resembled it until he began to look at prehistoric animals. He claims that the creature he saw that day was a pterodactyl. A while later, Edmond was hunting again in Bear Pen Hollow and saw a Herron fly above him. These are common to the area because of the lakes, and one might think he mistook the flying creature for one of these large birds. He says that the large Blue Herron could have been the flying creature's baby - that, in comparison, the Herron was minuscule to the thing he saw flying above him that day.

Edmond later heard from coal truck drivers and miners who worked at mines overlooking Martins Fork Lake that they had also seen giant birds like this in the same area. The one that Edmond saw and the ones that the miners saw were all flying toward Stone Mountain, which is southward and in the area of the Virginia/Kentucky border. Stone Mountain is known for cliffs, rock overhangs, and caves, which is a perfect habitat for giant creatures such as this.

The Pterodactyl, the common term for pterosaur, was a flying reptile thought to have been extinct 65 million years ago. The species met their demise around the same time as the dinosaurs when a comet or meteorite hit the earth—combined with volcanic eruptions changing the climate that supposedly killed off the pterosaurs.

Edmond and the miners may not be the first witnesses to a flying reptile millions of years after its supposed extinction. In 1890, a birdlike creature was reported to be similar to a pterodactyl in Tombstone, Arizona. This account made the local newspaper, the Tombstone Epitaph. Other reports of huge flying creatures have been reported throughout the years in many states across the U.S., suggesting that the elusive creatures may still exist.

Giant Ground Sloth

FOUND ON THE DESERT.

A Strange Winged Monster Discovered and Killed on the Huachuca Desert.

A winged monster, resembling a huge alligator with an extremely elongated tail and an immense pair of wings, was found on the desert between the Whetstone and Huachuca mountains last Sunday by two ranchers who were returning home from the Huachucas. The creature was evidently greatly exhausted by a long flight and when discovered was able to fly but a short distance at a time. After the first shock of wild amazement had passed the two men, who were on horseback and armed with Winchester rifles, regained sufficient courage to pursue the monster and after an exciting chase of several miles succeeded in getting near enough to open fire with their rifles and wounding it. The creature then turned on the men, but owing to its exhausted condition they were able to keep out of its way and after a few well directed shots the monster partly rolled over and remained motionless. The men cautiously approached, their horses snorting with terror, and found that the creature was dead. They then proceeded to make an examination and found that it measured about ninety-two feet in length and the greatest diameter was about fifty inches. The monster had only two feet, these being situated a short distance in front of where the wings were joined to the body. The head, as near as they could judge, was about eight feet long, the jaws being thickly set with strong, sharp teeth. Its eyes were as large as a dinner plate and protruded about half way from the head. They had some difficulty in measuring the wings as they were partly folded under the body, but finally got one straightened out sufficiently to get a measurement of seventy-eight feet, making the total length from tip to tip about 160 feet. The wings were composed of a thick and nearly transparent membrane and were devoid of feathers or hair, as was the entire body. The skin of the body was comparatively smooth and easily penetrated by a bullet. The men cut off a small portion of the tip of one wing and took it home with them. Late last night one of them arrived in this city for supplies and to make the necessary preparations to skin the creature, when the hide will be sent east for examination by the eminent scientists of the day. The finder returned early this morning accompanied by several prominent men who will endeavor to bring the strange creature to this city before it is mutilated.

Tombstone Epitaph, April 26, 1890

Pterosaur, commonly known as the Pterodactyl

The Creature at Old Cranks Lake

In the late 1970s and early 1980s, Edmond Gross frequently hunted the Cranks Lake area with his brothers and friends. The best hunting was at Bear Pen Hollow before you got to the Cranks Lake dam. Edmond was reluctant to hunt in the hollow because of a flying creature he had seen there once, but his brother, Mike, paid it no mind. He hadn't believed Edmond's account of the bird. Mike headed up Bear Pen Hollow on this day, and Edmond hunted on the road. Out of silence, Edmond suddenly heard Mike's semi-automatic rifle fire about three times. This was very odd, and Edmond wondered what Mike was doing. Typically, you do not fire a gun several times in a row at a squirrel. Edmond had turned around and was heading back to the truck when, all at once he heard a commotion. It was Mike running out of the hollow, shouting, "Get in the truck, get in the truck!"

Edmond asked Mike what was wrong when they were both in the truck. He told him he'd tell him later and to get them out of there. Edmond had to drive up to the dam and turn to leave, and as the truck passed the hollow again, Mike told him to speed up. Terrified, sweaty, and out of breath, Mike told him what had happened in the hollow. According to Mike, he had gone up the hollow to a cliff line where large hickory trees are. All at once, large trees on top of the cliff line began shaking violently, and whatever was shaking them began growling viciously. Mike shot up in the air to scare it away but instead angered it even more. Whatever it was started throwing boulders down at him, and as he ran away, it let out a piercing scream. Mike said he would never go into Bear Pen Hollow again, so both brothers hunted in the area but never that hollow after their experiences.

Edmond also heard other hunters tell of finding nests in Stone Mountain very near Bear Pen Hollow. The hunters claimed that near the cliff line, they found huge nests built in between several trees. The nests here are huge – much more extensive than an eagle's nest, but high up in the forest canopy. A couple of the hunters climbed the trees to investigate the nests. They reported finding deer skeletons and bones in them. They also said the nests had a horrible pungent odor about them. In the nearby rock ledges, bones and skeletons were also found. It seems they found the homes of very unusual creatures.

Edmond's oldest brother visited Bear Pen Hollow for the last time in the early 1980s. He also heard a roaring growl that made him never want to go into the hollow again, no matter how good the hunting was. Not long after that, Edmond's father's friend visited, and the two men were drinking coffee and talking. Edmond wasn't interested in the conversation until the man brought up Bear Pen Hollow. With piqued interest, Edmond began listening. The friend said that one night while coon hunting in the hollow, his two hounds caught a scent of something at the cliff line and went out of earshot around the ridge. It was autumn and getting chilly, so he built a fire while waiting on his dogs. Suddenly, he heard a howling scream, and his dogs came bolting out of the hollow. The two terrified dogs got between his legs and wouldn't move. He quickly kicked dirt on the fire to put it out, leashed his dogs in the back of his truck, and left.

The Martins Fork and Cranks area near Cranks Lake has had many different people experience sights and sounds that cannot be explained. Most who encounter this phenomenon vow never to return, while a few seem drawn to experience it again. Either way, Cranks Lake seemed steeped in mysteries yet to be solved.

Cranks Lake, Harlan County, Kentucky

Cliff line view from Cranks Lake on Stone Mountain.

The following stories were contributed by Chad Daniels, a lifelong resident of Harlan County.

The Wolf Hollow Creature

In the late 1980s, Chad was in his early 20s. During this time, he and four friends decided to go camping at Wolf Hollow near Loyall, Kentucky. The campsite was at Buzzard Rock, a popular campsite at Wolf Hollow. The young men began hiking to the site one evening around dusk and noticed high-pitched yelps they assumed to be coyotes while on their way. Thinking nothing of it, they continued on their way.

As they made their way up the mountain this summer night, a couple of young men were ahead of the rest of the group and began going the wrong way. Seeing they were disoriented, the remaining three began yelling at them to stop. As they did this, they heard what sounded like a much lower guttural call, unlike anything they had heard before. This time, the young men were frightened by what they heard and began running. When they felt it was safe to stop, they noticed one of them was no longer with them. Fearing they had left him behind, they began calling out to him. He responded ahead of them, and they were relieved to find he was not behind them.

Their relief was suddenly halted by another deep, loud howl that resonated through the woods. By this time, it was dark, and the young men panicked and began wildly descending the mountain, tumbling and falling the entire time. Finally, they were out of the mountain and felt safe again.

As they stood talking about what had happened, the two boys that had gone the wrong way said that the guttural growl they heard was very close to them. They had been about 20 yards ahead of the rest. One of the young men said that he looked back while running down the mountain, and he said that he saw glowing red eyes about ten feet high. He said that whatever he saw was either in a tree or extremely tall. All of them agreed that the creature had chased them down the mountain.

Chad says this creature was not a bear, and to this day, he does not know what it was that terrified him and his friends that summer night many years ago.

The Attack at Coal Stone Hollow

Chad had another unusual occurrence in the early 90s at a place in Bell County called Coal Stone near Balkan. Coal Stone Hollow and Black Snake Road led into the same place where he and his cousin were going to camp and bow hunt deer. This area was known as an excellent deer hunting area. This spot was so good for hunting that it was set up as a camping spot by deer hunters.

Chad and his cousin drove a pickup to this popular camping spot and planned to spend the night, wake up early, and begin hunting. They built a fire and were sitting and enjoying the night when they started hearing sounds. A rock came out of the woods and landed near them. They didn't pay much attention to the first rock, but they took notice as other rocks as large as a cantaloupe began hitting near the fire.

Chad quickly grabbed a rifle and fired several shots into the tree line, high in the air, to frighten away whoever was trying to bother them. He had assumed that some young people were trying to scare them. After the two men sat back down at the fire, Chad noticed how large the rocks were and how far they had traveled through the air. He thought to himself that whoever had thrown them had to have been of superior strength. Chad's cousin picked up one of the rocks, and although he was a weightlifter, he could only throw the rock about 20 feet. The stones had traveled between 30 and 50 yards. Chad was very puzzled about who could do this and do it multiple times. He also found it odd that he heard nothing and saw nothing, even with a spotlight. This camping spot was about three miles off of any main road. It would have been easy to hear a vehicle on the gravel road, and they would have seen headlights. He would have heard the leaves crackling this October night as the culprits ran away. Chad could not imagine why someone would sneak three miles back into the woods, throw rocks at them, and then leave.

Troubled by the unusual event with the rocks, Chad didn't sleep well that night. Just before daybreak, they arose and headed to their deer stands. The two men were finished hunting around noon and were eager to pack up and head out. Upon returning to the campsite, they were stunned by what they saw. Everything had been destroyed. Chairs were turned over, the tent had been shredded, and sleeping bags and backpacks had been strewn around. A huge wooden cable spool used for a table by everyone had been flipped and rolled down the hill, which was a remarkable feat of strength. These spools, used to store mining cable, are around 200 pounds. Although the entire campsite had been vandalized, Chad's truck had not been destroyed. He felt they probably would have tried to damage his vehicle if it were vandals.

As they tried to pick up their belongings, Chad never found the top of a cooler torn apart. He was baffled at the shape of the camping gear. The military-grade canvas tarp used to put over the tent was torn in ways that were a mystery. They were not cut with a knife, and it appeared they had been ripped by hand. He knew this was impossible to do. Chad knew the difference between rips and knife cuts, and the items had been torn apart by hand. During this time, bears were rare, and their motivation was food. The men had eaten their food the night before and for breakfast. There was no food left. Whatever did this seemed to be angry.

Chad and his cousin believe that something was trying to run them out of the campsite and was responsible for the rock attack and the vandalism. The question they have never answered is what it could be.

Daisy Cawood Woods

This occurrence happened after Chad was married and had children around 2000. He frequently hunted deer in Daisy Cawood Woods in the Catrons Creek area. There was a particular deer that he had hunted for several times. He always took a portable deer stand with him and set it up on this day, climbed in it, and began waiting for the deer. He had driven his four-wheeler in, parked about half a mile away. Cell phones were ineffective during this time, and his only form of communication was a CB radio on the ATV.

As he sat there quietly, he got the distinct feeling of being watched. He was totally alone, far back in the woods and camouflaged in the deer stand. He should have been entirely out of sight to anyone or anything, yet the undeniable feeling that he was being watched would not leave him. He scanned the area for something and saw nothing. He could hide himself so well in his stand that people had walked under the stand in the past and had never noticed him.

As he sat in silence, he also observed that the woods had been full of different sounds when he had first arrived. Birds had been singing, squirrels squawking, and bugs buzzing around, but now, it was eerily quiet. Chad then began to feel the hair stand up on his arms, and he knew something was not right, and felt apprehensive. He was so anxious that he began trembling.

After about an hour up in the deer stand, and with no relief from the dreaded feeling he was being watched, Chad decided to call it a day. He was not enjoying himself and could get no peace. He carefully climbed out of the tree stand, and when he was about 10 feet off the ground, he got the unshakeable urge to turn and look behind him. When he did, he saw a dark figure standing eye-to-eye with him. It quickly ducked behind the tree. Shaken by what he had seen, Chad ensured his gun was ready to fire. He got his stand and bow and promptly made his way to his four-wheeler, on high alert the entire time. Although he never saw the creature again, he still had the feeling of being watched until he drove his four-wheeler out of the woods.

Chad didn't feel normal until he reached Sunshine Hollow. Daisy Cawood Woods and Buzzard Rock are about half a mile away from one another. Chad always wondered if the creature he saw that day was the same one he and his friends encountered near Buzzard Rock many years ago. Although Chad has been in the woods his whole life and enjoys camping alone, he never went to Daisy Cawood Woods again.

Justin Flannery is a paranormal enthusiast and has joined us on many projects. The following events happened while living in Owsley County.

The Cryptid of Cowcreek

In 2011, Justin lived in a house with three lifelong friends in the Cowcreek community of Owsley County, Kentucky. One of his friends, Aaron, had enjoyed investigating the paranormal since they were kids. Aaron's brother, Steven, and cousin, Axel, lived with them.

Justin worked the night shift, so any errands needed were done in the evening before work. One evening, he realized it was time to go grocery shopping. He, Aaron, and Steven headed to the grocery store in London, Kentucky, which is about an hour and a half away.

The three were in Justin's 1999 Cavalier and were traveling through country wooded roads that were very isolated. It was about 10 or 11 p.m. when they approached the town of Booneville. Aaron was taking pictures with a digital camera and having fun. As they reach the top of a hill, they see a huge creature standing about 8 feet tall on the side of the road. It had white, shaggy fur and was stepping over a cattle fence with ease that was about four feet high.

Justin slowed down and wondered if he was the only person in the car seeing the creature until he heard Steven gasp in the backseat. He then realized this was not his imagination. The two stared in shock at this big bipedal being with a narrow snout and doglike features. It looked back at them with little concern and went about crossing the fence.

Meanwhile, and ironically, Aaron was not seeing this remarkable creature because he was playing with his camera in his lap. Not knowing if it was friendly or aggressive, Justin kept driving and passed by this beast and was only 10 feet away from it at one point.

Justin felt exhilarated yet fearful of this cryptid encounter he'd always dreamed of having. He claims that the experience made him feel alive and assured him that unknown things exist. However, being a skeptic and logically minded, he asked Steven what he saw. Steven then described precisely what he'd seen as well.

The duration of the trip was spent discussing their experience and telling Aaron what they had seen. When they got home, they searched the internet and discovered a similar creature – a white Sasquatch with a dog face- had been sighted in Appalachia on several occasions. Justin is still amazed that after searching for the unknown most of his life, he encounters it one night while simply making a trip to the grocery store.

Although Justin had always been interested and fascinated with all things paranormal, this event is why he gave it all up for nearly 15 years.

The Pink House Entity

The "Pink House" is a historic home in the Green Hall community of Jackson County, Kentucky. True to its name, the Pink House is bright pink. It is a Victorian-era home and sits just feet off the road. The Painted Lady has a history of being haunted, and Justin's grandmother actually lived there for a time when she was a child. She claims to have had the covers pulled from her bed while she slept, and dishes would come flying out of the cupboards and crashing to the floor.

After hearing the tales of the Pink House all his life, Justin decides to visit the house when he was about 19 years old. He spent most weekends ghost hunting, so he got his ghost-hunting gang together and planned an investigation at the Pink House. Justin, his best friend, Aaron, Aaron's oldest brother, Brian, their friend

Brandon, Aaron's cousin, Axel, and Justin's girlfriend at the time, headed out to the house in a hunter-green 1996 Geo Tracker.

They called themselves the Kentucky Ghost Research Team and were more than eager to investigate this legendary house. It was rumored that serial killer Donald Harvey, AKA The Angel of Death, had lived there once. Harvey was an orderly at Marymount Hospital in London, Kentucky, and is thought to have killed nearly 90 patients. Because of his possible connection to the house, it was suspected by Justin and his group that it could possibly have some very dark energy attached to it.

Upon arrival, Justin had difficulty finding a place to park due to its location on the roadside. The house was built before cars, and there had probably been a horse path in front of it at one time. He lets everyone out in front of the house and then finds a place nearby to park the car. Brandon decides he doesn't want to participate, so Justin tells him to wait in the car and pick them up when they are done. He then makes his way to the group already at the house. When he arrives, some of them are excited, telling him they have already had some experiences.

When they exited the car, they began taunting the spirits and acting silly. Suddenly, they heard a growling sound from the edge of the woods. They spy a large Tomcat glaring at them but also see a jet-black figure wandering around the property. They regret acting disrespectfully and foolishly and fully believe the house is haunted.

Although apprehensive now, they continue to investigate. They approach the front door, which was boarded up when they arrived. The boards were removed and neatly stacked in a pile next to the door. Justin asked the rest of the group if the door was indeed boarded up when they arrived. They said they, too, saw it boarded up.

The night was something out of a horror movie, with fog lying heavily on the ground at a haunted farmhouse in the middle of nowhere. The door was now open, so they decided to push on and investigate as they had intended. Meanwhile, Brandon and Justin's girlfriend drive the Tracker around to find a better place to park.

Aaron goes first and reaches for the front door. It's as if time stands still in that moment because from around the door comes long, bony fingers clenching to the doorframe. Stooping down to look through the doorframe is a face with white paper mâché looking skin and tiny beady eyes. There is a slit for the nose and no hair on its white head. It had no ears or lips. As it ducks down to look out the door, it grins, shows needle-sharp teeth, and looks at the boys. In a fight or flight reaction, Justin grabs Aaron and wildly begins running toward the Tracker they see coming in the distance. He jumps a fence with Aaron, and they are all in a panicked, terror-stricken shock. The entire time, Justin is praying to Saint Michael for protection because he feels the malice, hate, and evilness emitting from the presence.

The group is running toward the car with all their might. They hop in, and Justin throws Aaron in like he's luggage. The hatchback is flung open, and Brandon jumps in the back. Justin gets in and steps on the gas, and the car won't go over five miles per hour. He floors the gas pedal, and it will not budge past 55 miles per hour. The boys in the hatch back first notice a blue light that exits the pink house and is approaching them. Justin then sees it from his rearview mirror, and everyone in the car can now see it.

Suddenly, Aaron exclaims that he has been hit with something in the back of the head. At that point, the car can now accelerate to full speed and go from 55 to 80 in seconds. The blue light disappears, and they speed all the way home. Wrecking was better than spending another second with that monster.

A couple of days later, Brandon was driving his car with Justin, Axel, Aaron, and Brian riding with him. They lived in Owsley County and were driving around the back roads. They were all talking and having a good time when the car's energy suddenly changed. Brian was the first to say, "Guys, I think I feel death is in this car." At that point, everyone feels it. They became quiet and started looking around.

Aaron puts both hands on his knees, spine straight, and looking down at the floor. He claims he is angry and started saying it over and over. No one knows what is happening with him, but then the energy changes back, and Aaron returns to normal. While acting strangely, he said his vision changed, and he viewed everything through what seemed like a red lens. He was trapped in his own body. He was trying to tell them that something was wrong but could not.

They call it a night and go home to decompress after these disturbing events. Justin felt the evil entity may have attached itself to Aaron and was letting them know it was still with them. He was one of the ones who acted disrespectfully and the only one who got hit with something in the head.

The next day, Brandon picks up Brian and Aaron to go to Jackson, Kentucky, in Breathitt County to eat and do some shopping. They stop by Justin's house and ask him to go, telling him they are going to GameStop and to the Mexican Restaurant, which typically is a trip he wouldn't miss. However, something kept telling him not to go. He tells them to go ahead and is unsure why, but he is confident he is not supposed to go.

Later that night, in the same Cavalier they were driving the night before, the same group except Justin gets in an accident. They were going on an isolated road when suddenly they wrecked and began rolling. They rolled over a hill, and when it came to a stop, they all crawled out. They then noticed that a tree had gone through the exact spot where Justin always sat and where he would have sat had he gone with them. Undoubtedly, he would have been killed if he had not listened to the voice in his head. Justin feels certain that it was the work of the evil entity. It was targeting him because he had cried out to Saint Michael, the ultimate mighty warrior, possibly preventing it from doing harm that night at the Pink House.

Justin describes the feeling of that encounter of being in the same room with a serial killer. He says they were the mice, and the cat was the evil entity. It could literally do anything it wanted with them. Although many years have passed, Justin feels that even today, he sometimes feels a lingering presence of the evil entity of the Pink House. The experience with the evilness that dwells inside the Pink House changed Justin forever.

The prayer of Saint Michael:

"Saint Michael the Archangel, defend us in battle. Be our protection against the wickedness and snares of the devil; May God rebuke him, we humbly pray; And do thou, O Prince of the Heavenly Host, by the power of God, thrust into hell Satan and all evil spirits who wander through the world for the ruin of souls. Amen."

This story was contributed by Nick Sturgill, director of Portal 31 in Lynch, Kentucky.

The Giant Rattlesnake Snake of Black Mountain

Rattlesnakes grow unusually large in Harlan County. A snake killed a few years ago in Wallins Creek, Kentucky, was so big that its tail was dragging the ground on one side of a Ford pickup truck, and its head was dragging the ground on the other. Many estimated this snake to be over 10 feet long, two feet larger than the most giant rattlesnake on record, which is 7'9" long and weighs 34 pounds. According to eyewitnesses, it was as big around as a man's thigh, and its head was bigger than a man's fist.

There is another account of a massive rattlesnake at a coal mine in Louellen, Kentucky, which is in the Highsplint area of Harlan County. A mechanic working at the garage of the mines said he was in the garage and heard something outside. He looked out and saw an enormous rattlesnake going up into the mountain. He said he was unsure how large it was, but it took a very long time before all of it slithered out of sight.

According to Nick's grandfather, in the early 20th century, when powerlines were first being installed across Black Mountain, a lineman was pulling himself up the side of a cliff when a giant rattlesnake attacked him. The snake was so huge that the man's entire head was in its mouth. Terrified and panicked, the man pushed away with all his might, fell off the cliff, and landed on the ground below. It was unknown if the fall or the snake bite killed him, but the man died on the spot.

After the linesman fell to his death, his coworkers climbed the cliff to find the monstrous snake. The massive creature was making its way down the side of the mountain, and the men pulled out their guns and began shooting at it. The bullets didn't seem to affect the creature, and it slowly slithered down the mountains, breaking trees and bushes that snapped under its enormous weight. The snake was never found, and the bullets did not penetrate its leathery, tough skin.

Nick had forgotten the tale of the gigantic rattlesnake when, nearly 30 years later, his father-in-law told a similar story. His father-in-law said that his mother had saved a newspaper article from long ago telling about the linesman being attacked and killed by a colossal snake on Black Mountain near Lynch, Kentucky. He recalled the article being from the 1920s. The article told the same story Nick's grandfather had told and even included the fact that the snake had been shot multiple times but was never harmed by the bullets.

Although this story is horrifying, the most frightening part is that the snake got away. Normal rattlesnakes can live 20 years or more, but this was not an ordinary snake. It is possible that this snake lived and reproduced for decades. Many modern-day accounts of exceptionally large snakes are found in Harlan County, with some being over 6 feet in length. Although these snakes would be tiny compared to the one estimated at around 20 feet long, one must wonder if these are the descendants of the massive snake of Black Mountain. Even more worrisome is the possibility that more of these gargantuan snakes still live in the dense forests of Harlan County.

Eastern Diamondback Rattlesnake

Uktena – The Giant Serpent

In our previous story, we told the tale of a massive rattlesnake that supposedly killed a man in the 1920s on Black Mountain. When electricity first came to the area, linemen were enlisted to install power lines. One of these linemen was supposedly attacked by a snake so huge that it could put the man's entire head in its mouth. The terrified lineman fought for his life and broke free from the serpent, unfortunately falling from the cliff on which he had been working. Other linemen attempted to shoot the giant snake, but it slithered back into the deep forest of Black Mountain, perhaps searching for another victim.

According to Cherokee legend, Uktena (Ook-tay-nah) is an enormous snake with horns and a diamond on its forehead that glows like a light. It lurks in the highest peaks of mountains, waiting to lure its victims with its mesmerizing light. Pine Mountain, the second-highest peak in Kentucky and neighbor to Black Mountain is said to be home to this legendary creature. Although this sounds fanciful, it's quite possible that Uktena was spotted in the summer of 2019.

Zac Caudill and Michael Amburgey were in the woods near Lewis Creek around the Harlan County/Letcher County line. Michael loves snakes and owns many that he keeps as pets and for educational purposes. At nightfall, their search led them to a cliff line that, according to Zac, was so steep it was merely a rock wall with no incline – a straight drop-off. Humans or animals couldn't travel on this terrain. As they continued, both noticed a diamond light flickering on the side of the cliff. They watched as the glow would dim and then brighten again. Too high for their flashlights to reach, they continued to watch, bewildered at what could possibly be on the rock wall.

Both agree that if it were daylight, they might have seen the gargantuan serpent, Uktena, slithering around the side of the cliff. One must remember that they were searching for snakes. Uktena may have wanted to give them the snake encounter of a lifetime.

This story was contributed by Steven Ray.

The Giant Rattlesnake of Smith, Kentucky

In the late 90s, Steven and his parents decided to take the scenic route from Smith to Middlesboro on an infrequently traveled road. Highway 987 goes from Smith to Bell County and is a relaxing, beautiful drive.

Well into the trip, the Blazer hit something that appeared to be a log in the road. They were shocked when the log began moving. At that point, they realized it was not a log they ran over but a colossal snake sunning itself on the warm pavement.

Steven's dad quickly turned in the road and returned for a better look. Inching its way to the ditch was a massive rattlesnake with 19 rattles and a button. It was around 20 feet long and 12 inches in diameter. Steven's dad ran to the Blazer, got his 38, and shot it in the head twice with little to no effect on the snake.

They then drove to a nearby trailer park and told a man working outside about the snake. He got a sawed-off shotgun, and they ran back to the snake. The man shot in a couple of times, severing it in half.

The halves were then stretched out over the Blazer, and both ends of the halves touched the ground on both sides. They were all in disbelief at the length of the massive rattlesnake. It was easily 20 feet long.

Steven hasn't seen a snake remotely that large since that day, back in the summer of 1998, when he saw the giant rattlesnake of Smith, Kentucky.

UFO Landing at Slope Hollow

Slope Hollow is a connector of Big Black Mountain in the Cumberland area and Little Black Mountain in the Evarts area of Harlan County. Both are the same mountain range but are distinguished by "Big and Little," with "Big" being the tallest peak. Slope Hollow is home to many unexplained phenomena, one being an unidentified flying object that descended upon it.

In the winter of 2012, Zac Caudill was a senior in high school. He lived in Cumberland and walked daily to the school bus stop with his sister. On this day, his sister was sick, so he was by himself waiting for the bus. It was then that he noticed a large oblong object in the sky with three bright lights on it.

Soon, the bus pulled up, and Zac got on without saying anything about what he saw. As he sat down, he realized the object was still hovering in the sky. He went up to his bus driver and pointed it out to him. The bus driver said it must be a UFO. The bus then stopped to pick up another student, Nick. Zac showed Nick the flying object, and Nick called his mom and told her to look at it. It wasn't long before his panicked mother was behind the school bus. She told Nick to tell the bus driver to pull over. Nick's mother got him off the bus and took him back home because she was frightened of the UFO and what it might do next.

Zac then decided to call his mother and tell her not to let his sister stay home alone. He told her to go out and look and see if the object was still there. Zac's mother told him she had seen it landing in the area of Slope Hollow. The huge disc-shaped object slowly descended into the tree line.

Zac claims that the UFO he saw that winter morning is the most amazing thing he's ever seen. It must have also left an impression on the bus driver as well because, on the very last day of school, the bus driver wished Zac well and told him goodbye. He also told Zac that he would never forget the day they saw the UFO flying above Cumberland.

The Cabins on the Hill

Near the community of Woodland Hills in Harlan, Kentucky, there is a pair of lovely cabins by a pond tucked away high on a ridge. Although very secluded now, it was once a community with houses and markets. Horses, carriages, and foot traffic used a primitive road. One of the only remnants of this early settlement is a cemetery with tombstones dating back to the 1800s.

The two cabins were used for work purposes, vacation homes, and rental properties. The owners of the cabins have had problems with their tenants staying, with some breaking leases to leave. Many people who visit there have unnerving experiences of the haunted nature.

Strange sounds can be heard, shadows creep through the house, and sometimes ghostly apparitions can be seen. The homes and the area around them have had their share of tragedies, with several suicides and shootings occurring there. It is speculated that this is the reason for the hauntings.

That, however, may be different. A firsthand account of seeing a full-body apparition may prove otherwise. Steven Ray, who is employed in animal rescue, used to work for the owners of the cabins and property. He was often required to do maintenance there.

One day, he and a co-worker were doing some repairs at the cabins. It was a lovely day, and they decided to have lunch outside. They noticed a woman peering out the window of one of the cabins as they ate. She gazed down at them with a somewhat blank stare.

Knowing that no one should be in the house, they jumped up quickly and searched the house – no one was there. They went back out and began reflecting on what they had just seen. The woman appeared elderly, with gray hair and a bun on her head. She wore a white button-up blouse with puffed sleeves. It didn't take long for Steven to realize that this woman was not of their era. She was wearing fashion from the late 1800s.

The early settlers of that land may haunt the cabins. The tragedies could also result from paranormal activity, but the people who first inhabited the property are still there, ensuring their land is cared for properly.

UFO Caught on Camera

Belinda Taylor is a talented and skilled photographer. She has taken over one million photographs during her life. Because of her experience and expertise, she became the lead photographer during Tony's many paranormal investigations.

Besides photographing to capture paranormal evidence, Belinda also enjoyed taking still photos of Tony and the team and candid shots of them having fun. She always had her camera and nearly always snapped pictures of everything around her. Her photography was a huge part of her life, and it shows in the beautiful and detailed pictures she took.

During the paranormal investigations, the rule was to take all photographs in threes. This is to ensure the validity of a photograph. Belinda tended to keep this format during all her photography, whether during an investigation or not.

One day, while exploring Black Mountain, which happens to be the highest peak in the state of Kentucky,

Belinda and Tony decided to do an impromptu photo shoot. She had Tony sit on a rock that would show the beautiful mountain range in the background. She quickly snapped three pictures, and then they went on with their exploration.

It wasn't until Belinda downloaded the photos on her computer that she noticed something odd in the second photo of Tony. It was a large, shiny, bell-shaped object in the background. She claims that she did not see the object while taking the photos. Of the three photographs taken, only the second photo has this odd image. It is as if the camera caught something moving so quickly that the naked eye could not see it.

This is not the first account of a UFO on Black Mountain. Through the years, many people claimed to have witnessed mysterious objects in the sky on this tall mountain summit.

Photograph of Tony Felosi taken by Belinda Taylor on Black Mountain in Harlan County, Kentucky. The mysterious object hovers in the background.

The Ghosts of Portal 31

Nick Sturgill is the director of Portal 31. Portal 31 opened on November 2, 1917. It was the crown jewel of the Lynch, Kentucky, mining industry. It was the largest mine, produced the most coal, had the most miners working there, and, unfortunately, had the most fatalities. Between 160 to 180 men have been killed in Portal 31, and a plaque is outside the mine honoring those who lost their lives. In the area of the coal mine that is now the tour, nine men lost their lives due to rock falls or mining car accidents.

One tragic story is that of Camillo Favaro, an Italian immigrant who began working in Portal 31 in 1926. Mr. Favaro worked in Portal 31 for 30 years; in 1956, he was ready to retire. On his last day of work, as he walked out of the mines for the last time, he noticed a shovel on one of the tracks at the entrance. He walked over to pick it up and was run over by an out-of-control coal car and killed. Mr. Favaro's son visits Portal 31 and the deathplace of his father every year.

Portal 31 is now a tourist attraction and open to the public. The part of the mine included in the tour is one of the oldest sections and was mined from late 1917 to August 1918. Thousands of tourists visit Portal 31 yearly to experience a taste of what it was like to work in the dark, damp coal mines of Eastern Kentucky.

Before working at Portal 31, Nick was a skeptic of the paranormal, but starting from day one, he changed his outlook completely. It began with strange feelings but soon progressed to hearing voices that ranged from a single person to groups of men talking. The voices would occur when no one was there except Nick.

Music can also be heard in Portal 31. The music is described as big band or jazz, which would have been popular in the first half of the 20 th century. Nick's wife has also heard the music. One day after work, his wife, Tessa, joined him inside the mine and was very startled when she began hearing the music. Tessa claims that she heard a piano playing from far back in the mine.

Things are frequently moved from where the employees leave them. It is nearly a daily occurrence that Nick gets a tool from its designated spot only to find it missing. The tool is usually found randomly in the mine, and many times, these tools were put up by Nick himself.

In 2019, Nick was working late at night at Stop Two when he heard someone say, "Hey, Buddy!" It sounded like an older man with a gruff voice calling out. At first, Nick thought someone else had entered the mine, but then he remembered it was 11:30 at night, and the gates were locked. He looked all around, inside and outside the property, but no one was there.

A mantrip is the vehicle miners use to go deep into the mine and now is used to transport visitors on the tour. This car runs along a track throughout the mine. Sometimes, when the mantrip is not operating, Nick can still hear the thunderous-sounding vehicle running on the steel tracks. Other times, he hears clanging that sounds like someone working on the tracks.

Tracks must be sanded for traction, and sand must be sprinkled on them to absorb moisture and prevent spinning. Nick sands the tracks every day that the Portal is in operation. He typically sands the tracks every evening, but one evening, he didn't have time. He filled his sand bucket and planned on sanding the track first thing in the morning. The following day, although he was the first to arrive, he found the track sanded. The procedure is to sand one section of the track, and all the employees know that. The sand, however, was on every inch of track in Portal 31, which is never done. Nick asked another employee if he did it, and he jokingly replied, "Maybe some of the old timers needed some traction."

Mysterious lights can also be seen in Portal 31. Nick and others have seen lights flickering throughout the mine that are not part of the tour. Although there are several light sources in the mine tour, there are no moving lights, but moving lights that look like a handheld lantern or mining cap light can be seen occasionally. The lights have also been seen by tourists attending the tour. Visitors to the mine have asked about moving lights, but there isn't an explanation for them.

Walking tours were offered in 2019 while the mantrip was getting repaired. During one of these walking tours, there were about 20 visitors, with half adults and the other half children. At Stop Six of the tour, Nick began talking about that particular section of the mine, when a child about six years old raised his hand and asked who the little boy was. Nick was confused and didn't know what the child meant. Nick asked the little boy to explain. The little boy's father stood behind him and said, "Who is the man and little boy walking down the tunnel?" and pointed toward Stop Five. Other group members began speaking up and said that they had seen a man dressed in typical mining attire holding hands with a small boy walking around in the mine. Most thought it was part of the tour and that they were employees dressed up for added effect, but this was not the case. About a dozen people in the group saw this ghostly man and boy. Nick noticed the group looking behind him often and wondered what they saw. He knew that no one was inside the mine dressed in that attire and was certain that the group had seen the apparition of a man and boy.

Sometimes, there is fog in Portal 31 in the morning due to moisture and weather. This is common, especially in the summer. There is, however, a mysterious fog that is not a result of the weather. Unlike the typical fog, this fog moves from place to place in the mines. One employee witnessed the fog coming toward him and against the ventilation, which should have been impossible. If it were typical fog, it should be pushed away from the ventilation, not going toward it.

Rocks being thrown are a common occurrence. This has happened to many employees, including Nick. Sometimes, they are tossed forcefully, while other times, they are tossed lightly, landing in front of them. This happens frequently near Stop Three.

No one seems to fear Portal 31 because the spirits who live there mean no harm. They want to be helpful and go about their duties of yesteryear. Many tragedies occurred here throughout the years; sometimes, a life could end instantly without warning. Perhaps some of the spirits do not realize that they have passed on. They are going about their work without the knowledge that their lives ended many years ago.

Portal 31, Lynch, Kentucky

The Hellhound of Little Black

Russell Sutherby was squirrel hunting in Evarts, Kentucky, in a hollow where the Peabody Mine used to be. Once a thriving coal mine, it now sits in silence, the forest taking over with vines and trees. The mine is at the foot of Little Black Mountain, and Russell had made his way there just a little before daylight and was under scaley bark trees, ready for the squirrel to begin stirring.

He was standing under a small tree watching for squirrels when a pebble hit the ground beside him. A few seconds later, another landed in the exact same spot as the other. Thinking someone was playing a trick on him, he looked around to see who was there but saw no one.

As daylight approached and he could see better, Russell noticed the opening of the old coal mine. As he stared at the opening, to his shock, a huge black dog emerged from the old mine. It was solid black, with even its eyes being as black as coal. Terrified by the creature, Russell quickly reached for his rifle, but before he could aim, the dog disappeared.

A few years later, Russell, his uncle, and his uncle's friend were squirrel hunting at the exact location. They were near the old mine's shop building when their hunting dog began to run toward something. To his surprise, the hunting dog was running toward the same big black dog he had seen years ago. The hunting dog ran toward the massive beast, and as it approached it, the huge black dog smacked at the dog just like a human would. Unharmed, the terrified hunting dog ran back toward the men and passed them by, getting away from the giant dog as fast as it could. As the men stood staring at the black dog, it seemed to simply disappear once again. The man with Russell and his uncle quickly said that they had just seen a ghost dog.

The area around the old mine has a dark and eerie feeling. Men often lost their lives there, with many of the dead still remaining there today. It is a mystery as to why the black dog stays there, but all who have seen it say that it is a creature they have never seen before.

Tracks at Bill's Branch

In 2018, around the first of September, in Evarts, Kentucky, in a place called Jewel Ridge close to Blue Diamond Mine. Russell Sutherby and his friend were there to shed hunt, which is looking for antlers that elk and deer shed. They had found some nice antlers there before, so they decided to go there once again. As soon as they got into the valley, they could hear something up on the ridge line above them. It sounded like a roar mixed in with a scream and could make your hair stand on in. It caused a vibration that radiated throughout the valley. They heard it all around the ridgeline until it finally dissipated. The sound was on terrain that would have been impossible for humans to maneuver. Whatever was making the sound was briskly moving around the rocky ledges with ease. It was very surefooted and very fast, as well as knowing the area very well. Both Russell and his friend are experienced woodsmen, and they have never heard anything like it. It was neither a bear nor a cat. They felt as if they were being warned to leave the area, so they quickly headed to their truck and went home.

Russell and his friend, Lane Hensley, were at Bill's Branch in the Smith, Kentucky area about ten years ago. They would go to this particular place to deer hunt, shed hunt, and look for ginseng. At times, they would smell an unusual musky smell, and once, something huge chased them out of the woods.

In early 2023, Russell and Lane went to a deer stand in Bill's Branch and noticed huge bipedal footprints on their way. The prints in the mud were in a straight line and sometimes seemed to slide a bit. The large footprints seemed very humanlike and were in no way a bear track that Russell had seen many times.

The tracks led to a large tree, and something unusually tall had been scraping the bark off a tree. It was near this tree where Russell took a photo of one of the prints with his phone.

Footprint taken at Bill's Branch, 2023.

Sounds in the Woods

Lane Hensley was in the woods at Yancy, Kentucky, with his father and brother-in-law. The three men were crossing over into the Martins Fork Lake area when Lane's dad went to look at something hanging from a tree. It was then that they began to hear something running through the woods. Something at a high rate of speed seemed to be tearing its way through the forest and possibly toward the men.

Without looking back or thinking, a panic-stricken Lane took off running. Suddenly, his brother grabbed him and pushed him to the ground. He would have run off a cliff if he had not been pushed down. The sound disappeared, and they could not find a source for the brisk running they heard.

Another time at Yancy, Lane heard the sound of a man being attacked. The screaming voice wailed in pain and fear. People living nearby also heard it and called the police. No one could find the source of the horrible screams, even though local men thoroughly searched the woods. Since then, the phantom screams have been heard three more times.

Once, Russell was hunting for ginseng at Railroad Gap on Laden's Trail on Pine Mountain. He was in an isolated area when he began hearing the sound of children playing. He could hear two children having a conversation. He went to the exact spot where the sounds were coming from and continued to hear the sounds even though nothing was there. He headed out of the woods and went to where his truck was parked at the only place wide enough for vehicles. His truck was the only one there. Russell never figured out how children could have been so far up in the mountains without adults or vehicles.

These are several examples of unusual sounds that are heard in the mountains of Harlan County. Tales of unusual sounds go back hundreds of years to the present day.

The Leprechaun of Log Mountain

In 1999, when Heather was 14 years old, she visited an older couple in a neighborhood called Woodland Hills in the Log Mountain area of Bell County with a friend's family. Log Mountain is between the towns of Pineville and Middlesboro.

Heather, her friend, and her parents had visited for a while and were preparing to leave. The older couple walked them outside, and they were saying their goodbyes under a carport. It was a typical "Appalachian Goodbye" that lasted for quite a while. Heather and her friend wandered the yard and sat enjoying a beautiful evening.

It was at dusk – getting dark, but still daylight. They were sitting in the grass of the subdivision talking when they spied something on the neighboring house's roof. At first, they assumed it was a squirrel, but on further observation, they realized it was not.

The first thing they noticed was that the creature on the roof was not moving like a squirrel and, in fact, wasn't moving like an animal. It seemed to be walking upright on two legs and had a human-like gait. This sparked their attention, and they began diligently watching. They even stood up to get a better look.

The thing on the roof was on the farther side, so they could only see a portion of it. They could see the silhouette of its head and noticed that the top was perfectly flat. Whatever it was, it had a deliberate project going on. It was as if it were carrying something from one spot to another, perhaps picking something up and moving it. At other times, it appeared to be eating something. Whatever the thing was, it paid the girls no mind and continued with its tasks.

As the girls watched, the thing on the roof moved higher up on the pitch to where they could now see most of it. To their surprise, it was a small man of about three feet in height. He wore a top hat, a jacket, short trousers, and boots or stockings. Its face was not wholly human-looking, as its features were more sharp, gruff, and troll-like. It had a beard with very pronounced chin.

When the girls got a good look at what appeared to be a tiny man, they quickly jumped up and ran to the adults. They told them to look at what was on the roof, but by the time they did, the small man must have figured out he had been spotted, so he was making his way down the other side and hopping off and out of sight.

After the little man had gone, the girls agreed that he looked like a leprechaun. Although his outfit was not bright green but more earth tones, he had the complete look of a traditional Irish leprechaun. Even today, Heather says that is the only accurate way to describe what they saw.

Although it was many years ago, Heather is still in awe that she saw a leprechaun on a roof in Bell County, Kentucky.

The Black Mountain Devil Dog

Terry, or "Dr. T" as he prefers to be called, belonged to an adult softball league in 1974 representing his hometown of Lynch. This was an impressive team that rarely lost, and it was no surprise when they won first place overall in their league tournament. Terry was a great athlete and a martial arts expert. He claimed to have "not been afraid of anything." That is, until this particular night.

To celebrate their victory, the team was going over Black Mountain to Appalachia, Virginia, where one of the teammates was from and where the victory party was being held. Several young men had girlfriends living in Appalachia, so the entire team fit into four cars and headed to the party.

That night after the party, the four carloads headed home to Lynch and began the trip back across Black Mountain. Terry was driving the last car in the line, a 1972 442 Oldsmobile. This was a car that he claimed "could fly." His music played loudly, and everyone enjoyed the ride home.

Suddenly, the music stopped, and the other men in the car began asking Terry why he turned it off. Terry hadn't touched the stereo and quickly began trying to turn the music back on, but it acted as if it had stopped playing.

They heard what sounded like a large growl as they approached a curve on the mountain. Nonetheless, Terry continued to try to fix his stereo. They went around a curve and approached an area of the mountain where the road was broken off. Terry then noticed that his car was losing power.

Terry was still trying to figure out what was wrong with his car when he looked up to see a massive dog walking toward them. The dog bumped into the side of the car, growled, and stood there looking down at Terry. There were three other dogs that were also exceptionally huge. They, too, growled at the men.

This big red and gray dog had bright red glowing eyes with a head bigger than a pumpkin. It had sharp, pointy ears resembling horns and three-inch-long teeth. Inside, its mouth glowed blood red. It stood five feet tall and weighed about 300 pounds. This creature was looking Terry right in the eyes. The other dogs stood behind the largest one.

Terry tried desperately to speed away, but the car wouldn't get out of second gear, so it slowly pulled away from the dogs. He looked at the evil pack of dogs in his rearview mirror. To his horror, those dogs followed behind him for nearly a quarter of a mile. Finally, the music suddenly blasted back on, and the car regained power. Terry stepped on the gas and got away from the dogs.

They went about a mile when they met the other cars in the group ahead of them. They had pulled off to the roadside and were waiting on Terry because they were too afraid to go back for him. When they saw Terry's car, they jumped out of theirs and began shouting and asking if they had seen the dogs. The young men in the vehicles before Terry's were terrified and said they had just seen the devil. That is how Terry came to name the creature the "devil dog." The other carloads had the same experience as Terry's car. Their music stopped, the cars had mechanical trouble, and then, of course, they encountered the dogs. Everyone was utterly horrified.

Terry "Dr. T" Tinsley is now 67 years old, and he says that he still never crosses Black Mountain without a gun in the car in fear of the Devil Dog. He refused to cross the mountain alone for over a year and a half after this experience. He had never seen anything like the terrifying beast he saw that night so long ago. It was the most horrifying thing that he had ever experienced. He says he has heard the tale of Headless Annie and others about ghosts and apparitions on Black Mountain, but he has never seen any of those. However, he says he came face to face with the Black Mountain Devil Dog.

This story was shared by a man who wishes to remain anonymous.

The Massive Dog of Slope Hollow

Darren worked at a coal mine in the Evarts area of Harlan County. Because he lived in Cumberland, the quickest route to work and back was over Slope Hollow, which crosses Little Black Mountain and connects the two communities. It is scarcely traveled and in relatively rough condition in some areas. ATVs and work trucks are the only consistent traffic on the road.

In 2003, Darren worked in the mines from 3 pm to 11 pm. He was always anxious to get home and set out in his Silverado truck, which he used mainly for work travel. It was a cold February night, and he was trying to beat the snow that had been forecasted. He was maintaining a cautious yet steady speed across the rough terrain. As he neared the highest elevation of the trip, the damp road began to freeze, so he slowed down even more.

As he continued the long journey home, he noticed snow clouds starting to form, blocking the moonlight. It was a crisp, beautiful night, and the glow of the moon and stars had made visibility very easy. Darren knew snowfall would be coming soon.

Up ahead, he saw something on the side of the road. He was familiar with every inch of the road and knew this was unusual. Surely, someone wasn't walking this time of night in the brutal cold. As he approached it, his headlights glowed on what appeared to be a large dog. Dogs aren't unusual on Slope Hollow, but this wasn't a typical dog.

Darren gazed in amazement at the size of the creature. It was as tall as a man while sitting down. He came to a stop and stared at the huge beast. It was black and resembled a Doberman Pinscher with sharp pointy ears and a long snout. It was looking directly back at Darren, and he became somewhat apprehensive. He slowly reached for his pistol in the glove box without taking his eyes off the dog.

Not sure what to do, Darren decided he must drive past the dog and get home. Snow was coming soon, and he surely didn't want to get stuck on the mountain with the gigantic dog. He kept reminding himself that he was safe in the locked truck with a pistol. That eased his mind, but not entirely. This beast was intimidating, with its piercing black eyes looking directly at him.

As the truck slowly neared the creature, Darren was anticipating it moving or running away – it did not. He got over as far as he could without going into the ditch to avoid the dog, which wasn't moving an inch. It just kept staring into the cab of the truck at Darren.

As he passed by the dog, it peered in the driver's side window at him, mere inches from his face. Fear was taking over, and he was preparing to slam on the gas and escape as fast as possible. He slowly turned his head toward the dog, and its eyes seemed to pierce his soul. He began trembling and froze with fear. Suddenly, the dog leaped over the truck's cab and landed in the ditch on the other side. It turned and glanced at him once more before heading over to the side of the mountain.

With that, Darren pressed the gas and quickly made his way over Slope Hollow. After he got home, he couldn't stop thinking about the dog. It had to have been over six feet tall. It leaped from a sitting position over top of the truck's cab, which would be impossible for any animal. None of it made sense, and that was not an ordinary dog by any means. Sleep was impossible, as Darren lay in bed the rest of the night thinking about his experience.

Although it's been 20 years since Darren encountered the massive dog on Slope Hollow, he says he watches for it every time he crosses. He no longer works in the mines and usually crosses Slope Hollow for fun when the leaves are colorful during the fall. He says he will not travel that road at night or in an ATV because he knows there is a massive beast up there that he doesn't wish to encounter ever again.

Murder House

In Harlan County in the early 1980s, the brutal murder of a woman occurred, and to this day, it remains unsolved. Although robbery was the motive, most who remember it found it unthinkable that someone could harm the well-known and loved individual. It was a senseless murder because the woman, up in years, could not see well and had little physical strength left. She would have gladly given up her belongings in exchange for her life. The mystery of her killers still haunts her family and friends. There was no forced entry, and she wouldn't open the door to strangers. There must be a killer among them.

The beautiful old home the woman was murdered in came up for sale. Not being superstitious, David's dad felt it was an excellent opportunity to buy one of the nicest homes in the community. After the purchase, David and his family began working on the home, improving and updating it. David immediately felt uncomfortable inside the house but assumed it was because he knew of its gruesome past.

David was somewhat apprehensive when his father offered him the house instead of being elated. David decided to spend some time in the place to see if he could get used to it and become more relaxed there. It seemed to work, and he and his friends often went to the home in the evening to hang out and talk.

One night, he and a group of friends went to the house. A girl in the group asked if someone was already there. David told her there shouldn't be anyone there, and the girl responded that someone was looking out the window. David looked at the upstairs window, and sure enough, there was the silhouette of someone looking down at them. All four people in the group saw someone in the window.

David and another young man in the group quickly went to both doors, front and back, to see if they were locked, and they were. They assumed whoever was in there had locked the door behind them. David got his key and unlocked the front door. Whoever was in there was trespassing and had no business there. One of the girls in the group said she wasn't going inside and would wait by the front door.

David checked the downstairs thoroughly and found no one, so it was time to confront the trespasser upstairs. They went upstairs and first checked the bedroom where the silhouette was seen; no one was there. They then entered all the rooms upstairs, and the house appeared empty. David was now bewildered. With every light in the house turned on, he went through the house again with the same results. No one was there.

No one wanted to stay in the house now, so they went through turning off the lights and preparing to leave. As they walked downstairs, a chilling breeze came down the stairwell. David was the last one down, and suddenly, an invisible hand pushed all three of them, and they tumbled to the bottom of the stairs.

When the girl standing outside heard the commotion, she began running while the others burst out the door, leaving it wide open, sprinting to the car. After watching the house from the car for a few minutes, David got enough courage to go back in, turn the lights out, and lock the door. He and the other boy quickly went through the downstairs, flipping light switches and hurriedly closing the front door and locking it back.

They were backing out of the driveway when one of the girls shouted, "There they are!" In the streetlight's glow, someone in the upstairs window pulled the curtain back and looked at them. They then backed away, and the curtain fell into place again. David drove to a nearby gas station and called the police. The police searched the house and said there wasn't anyone inside the house.

David's family quickly sold the beautiful old home. David is sure that he and his friends saw someone, although it was proven that no one was there. The girl who stood watch outside said no one left the house. Someone or something pushed all three people down the stairs at once, and everyone there saw someone pull back the curtain and look at them as they were leaving. David's only explanation is that the elderly woman is still there, trying to protect herself and her home from her killers, who were never brought to justice.

The UFO Over Cumberland

George Brock, Jr. is called "Bud" among his friends and has lived in Bledsoe, Kentucky, near Leslie County most of his life. In 2010, he worked at Cumberland on a strip job for several years, and one Saturday morning, he had gotten some breakfast at Hardee's and was sitting in his truck eating before his shift started.

It was early morning, and at first, George thought the moon was still visible as it sometimes is in the early morning hours. Then, however, he noticed the giant sphere moving and floating across the sky rather quickly. As it moved across the sky, it passed across the moon, which ensured that George was not seeing the moon itself.

The moving sphere was above Highway 119 in the Oven Fork area and was traveling east. It went across the Apple Orchard and was approaching Black Mountain. Whatever this huge orb was, it was larger than the full moon it passed in front of. George sat and watched this floating object until it floated over Black Mountain and out of sight.

This was not the first time George had seen this unidentified flying object. In the mid-1970s, as a young boy, he was on Laden's Trail on the top of Pine Mountain when he noticed a vast round object floating above him. He could hear the wind-like sound that it made. This object would go back and forth and pass above him at least three times before floating out of sight. This sighting was near his last sighting, just off Highway 221 near the rock quarry at Gordon. George is unsure what he saw as a high school student and then again as an adult, but he is confident that it cannot be easily explained.

The following are the experiences of Dana Green.

Old Wheat Farm

In 1966, Dana lived on a farm in Winchester, Kentucky, in the community of Old Indian Fields. Her family rented a house called "Old Wheat Farm." They moved from Harlan when her dad got a job there. When the family moved in, they discovered the previous occupants had written on the wall, "We pity the ones who live here; strange things happen." That was an ominous way to see your home for the first time and seemed to be the precursor of a series of bizarre events. To add to the creepiness, their landlord had the upstairs padlocked, and they were only allowed to live in the downstairs part of the house.

Even though the message from the last residents was disturbing, Dana's family was in a tough place financially, and that was the only place they could afford. Dana, her parents, and five siblings had no choice but to continue settling in despite the warning and make the best of it.

On their farm, a big old tobacco barn stood in the field beside the house. They hadn't lived there long when Dana and her sister saw a hand waving from the barn window. They waved back, thinking it was someone they knew. The wave became a beckoning gesture, so the young girls got closer for a better look. To their shock, the hand and arm appeared disembodied and floating in mid-air. At that point, the girls didn't go any further. Almost every night, Dana or one of her siblings saw the snow-white hand waving to them from the barn.

After living there for a few weeks, moaning sounds would occur inside the house. Dana's mother, Dorothy, described it as someone in agony, crying as if they were dying. When the moaning began, Dorothy would get all the children together in the living room and have them sit on the couch to ensure they were safe. Dana still remembers how frightening it was sitting there listening to the terrible sound. The moaning mostly happened in the daytime when her dad was at work. Once, while the moaning occurred, the old-fashioned screen door split down the middle as if a knife or claw shredded the screen and then shattered the wood frame. To the family's terror, the door was ripped from the hinges and flung into the front yard. The mule tied up in the front yard jumped into the air and landed on its back, dead of fright.

Dana's older half-brother came to stay with them for a while. One morning before daylight, the moaning started at the old barn. Dorothy feared something had happened to her husband, who had just headed out on foot to work. She got Dana's fourteen-year-old half-brother and had him walk to the barn with her. The moaning was so terrifying that she turned to tell the boy to run, and he was halfway back to the house in a panicked sprint.

Dana and her family only stayed there one summer. Other animals began mysteriously dying, her brother took a severe fall from the barn loft, and they were isolated without a vehicle. Her grandfather insisted they stay with family and came and helped them move. He claimed that when he turned into the driveway on the morning of moving day, the temperature dropped 20 degrees, and he said, "The devil himself lives here."

Although Dana's family slept on the floor while staying with relatives, they were much happier being away from Old Wheat Farm. She claims no horror movie could represent their fear while living on that farm. She said she had never been more scared than when she lived there. Dana's brother returned to Old Wheat Farm many years later to see it again. The house is gone, but the old barn remains. Old Wheat Farm holds many secrets, and its dark past remains a mystery.

The Top Hat Man of Bardo Hollow

When Dana was a young girl, she and her family lived in a house at Bardo Hollow in the Catrons Creek area of Harlan County. She shared a bed with her sister, and one night, while they were lying in bed listening to their mother watch Adam 12, a popular television show at the time. Both girls, who were supposed to be asleep, were intently listening to the television show they so greatly wished they were watching. Because it came on late, listening to it was the best they could do.

Suddenly, a man leaned over the bed on top of Dana. He wore a black top hat and a black mustache and beard. He laughed a maniacal laugh and began twirling his finger in a spinning motion. Dana's mind started spinning wildly as if the man's hand had control of her brain. She began nudging her sister for help and asked, "Do you see that man?" Her sister responded that she didn't. Finally, the man disappeared, and Dana's severe dizziness subsided.

During her life, the top hat man visited Dana three times. Once at Bardo Hollow, once at Fairview in Harlan, and the last time was when she lived in Indiana. The same thing always happens: He comes to her in bed, laughs wildly, and begins spinning her in her mind. It has been many years since the top hat man has visited Dana, and she hopes he never does again.

Clarence The Ghost

In late 1979, Dana and her husband moved into their first apartment, the Buttermore Apartments, in the Buttermore Building on Main Street in Harlan. They felt very fortunate because it was one of the rare apartments that came furnished.

One night, she and her husband visited their friends, a couple who lived at Black Joe, which goes toward the Evarts area of Harlan County. While they were there, the toilet flushed by itself while all four of the young people there were sitting in the living room. The man who lived there laughed and said it was "Clarence," the ghost who lived there. He went on to tell them that Clarence plays pranks and hides things.

A few days later, similar things began happening at Dana's apartment. Toilets flushed, water would turn on, and things started disappearing. Once, Dana left her cigarettes on the arm of the chair to get a drink, and when she returned, they were gone. She pulled out the chair cushions, looked everywhere possible, and couldn't find the cigarettes. Furious, Dana shouts, "Clarence, I'm leaving the room, and when I come back, I want the cigarettes back where you found them!" She left, and when she returned, the cigarettes were back on the arm of the chair.

Clarence would turn pictures upside down on the wall and play other harmless pranks. Until one day, Dana went to the grocery store. It was a summer day, and when she came home, the heat hit her face when she opened the door. She discovered all four gas burners on the stove had been turned on, and the oven was on with the door open. Dana's friend was with her, and they turned everything off and turned the air conditioning on.

Later that evening, Dana's friend called her and told her that strange things were happening at her house. From then on, it seemed Clarence left with Dana's friend, and nothing more happened at the apartment. It appears that Clarence goes home with people and stays until another opportunity comes along.

The Nursing Home

Dana worked at a nursing home for ten years. She worked the night shift and had gotten close to many residents there. One of her favorites was an elderly man named Orville. Dana would pass out ice to the residents every night for their ice water. Orville would always get up when she came in so they could visit. She would see him in the reflection of the mirror as she got the ice and would ask him what he was doing up so late. This happened every time Dana came to work.

Sadly, Orville passed away one day. A couple of days later, Dana came into work and began to pass out ice as always. She saw Orville getting up in the mirror's reflection and thought nothing of it until she remembered Orville had died. She whirled around, but Orville wasn't there anymore.

Another time, while she worked at the nursing home, she noticed an elderly woman lying in bed, pointing up at the ceiling. Dana asked her what she was doing, and she said, "Don't you see those angels dancing around?"

Dana didn't see anything. A couple of hours later, she went to check on the lady, and she had died.

Two days later, another lady was in the same bed where the woman had died. She, too, asked Dana if she could see angels. Within several hours, that lady also died. The employees began calling that room "The Death Room."

Dana trained a new employee at the nursing home. It was a pretty young girl who worked the second shift. Dana worked the third shift, and one night, she heard someone whisper her name. She searched for who said it and never saw anyone. The new girl worked the second shift, and Dana worked the third. She would relieve the girl every night and take over for the rest of the night. One night at 11 p.m., Dana found the young girl trembling. She told Dana that something was whispering her name in the hall. Dana told her that the same thing was happening to her. Dana and the young woman had their name whispered often after that, and neither knew where it was coming from.

Time Warps on Black Mountain

Black Mountain is said to have mysterious powers and forces. For instance, the concept of time seems to be distorted there. The minerals deep within are creating magnetic fields, or possibly there is an energy field emitting from its vast depth. There are tales through the ages of people becoming disoriented and hopelessly lost. Some of the disappearances may be due to people becoming lost in time.

There are many accounts of time warps on Black Mountain. People say that time stands still, time is lost, or time does not move forward at a normal pace. One family saw the same mile marker over seven times before finally reaching the next one. At first, the mother started seeing the mile marker, then after about three times, one of the children in the backseat commented that the same marker had gone by several times. All five passengers in the car began watching as they passed the same mile marker five more times before reaching the next. As panic ensued, the mile markers began appearing in their normal descent.

On his way home from work, one lone traveler in Big Stone Gap, Virginia, headed up Black Mountain toward Benham at 9:37 PM. Depending on speed, it usually takes about 15 or 20 minutes to get over the mountain. The trip home was uneventful, and as he approached the country club at Lynch, he glanced at the clock in his car, which displayed 10:53 PM. Bewildered, he assumed the clock had malfunctioned. He looked at his phone, which also showed the same time. He arrived home to a concerned family with no logical explanation. He checked the gas in his car, and it hadn't used more fuel than usual. He still does not know where that hour of his life went or what happened.

Others claim to become hopelessly lost in areas of the mountain they are familiar with, and some people traveling on foot say that they pass by the same tree, rock, or landmark many times before finally getting out of the "loop." One can only wonder if the many missing people could be caught in a loop or time warp, desperately trying to return to the normal realm.

Highway 160 that goes over Black Mountain.

The Moth Creature of Lynch, Kentucky

Paul's grandparents lived in Lynch, Kentucky, on Creekside Road. While staying with his grandparents, he enjoyed visiting their neighbor, Bart Goins. Bart had a son, Ricky, and he and Paul attended school together and were friends. The home of Bart Goins was a hangout for the neighborhood children; often, the porch was filled with boys and girls stopping by to play and visit. Bart enjoyed the children and loved to tease and joke with them. He liked to play practical jokes on them, sometimes hiding their bikes when they weren't looking. Bart was a playful man whom the neighborhood kids all considered incredibly fun.

In the early spring of March 1976, Paul, Ricky, and several neighborhood girls were all at the Goins' home playing. They all congregated on the porch to rest, and Bart came out and sat with them. As Paul recalls, Bart's tone and demeanor were different than usual. He seemed serious and was not joking about what he was telling them.

According to Bart, he was driving his truck down Black Mountain toward Lynch on a recent night, and what he referred to as "a great white owl" flew toward and then over the top of his truck. He said that right before the giant, winged creature appeared, something that looked like "cigarette butts" began sprinkling down and hitting the windshield and hood of his truck. After these embers hit the truck, the most enormous, winged creature he had ever seen appeared in the distance. It flew toward him and glided over the top as it approached the truck. Bart had a full-sized Chevy truck, and he said its wingspan was so huge it covered his entire vehicle. As soon as he saw this white creature coming toward him, he put on his brakes and watched it fly over the top of the truck and out of sight.

Bart is now deceased, but Paul distinctly remembers this unusual experience he talked about long ago. The large white-winged creature resembles the now famed Mothman of Point Pleasant, West Virginia. Although described as an owl, Bart was utterly bewildered about what the creature actually was. The Mothman was credited with forewarning of impending doom, particularly the collapse of the Silver Bridge in Point Pleasant. The Scotia Mine Disaster struck on March 9, 1976, only days after Bart's experience. This coal mining tragedy is one of the largest in U.S. history, with the first explosion killing 15 coal miners and two days later, the second explosion killing 11 miners. Whether the two incidents are related is unknown, but Bart Goins had a remarkable experience on Black Mountain with a giant, winged creature.

This story was contributed by McKensi Johnson Gilliam. This occurrence happened to her grandfather and her aunt, Misty.

The Mothman of Slope Hollow

Slope Hollow is a remote area of Harlan County that crosses a portion of Black Mountain. It is an isolated, hard-to-access road that loggers and miners have traditionally used as a shortcut from Cumberland to Evarts, and currently is a favorite of ATV enthusiasts. Over the years, it was also a favorite spot for teenagers to go and hang out with their friends.

Misty and her friends wanted to find a place to go without being bothered by adults. The carload of young people went to the top of Slope Hollow and went about a mile down a side road that is rarely if ever, used.

 They all got out of the SUV and stood around talking and laughing when Misty's friend, Brooke, excitedly whispered, "Do you all hear that?" Everyone stopped talking and listened. From the night sky, they could hear what sounded like the wings of a bird flapping.

Suddenly, a vast dark silhouette that appeared to be a monstrous bird flew overhead. The panicked teenagers all ran for the vehicle. They piled into the SUV and began descending the mountain to Cumberland quickly.

To their horror, this giant birdlike creature followed them, flying above the SUV. They watched as this flying creature with a 10-foot wingspan glided and hovered above them.

Finally, about halfway down the mountain, the huge bird veered off and flew away. Everyone was silent for the rest of the way down. Back in the safety of Cumberland, they began talking about it and decided that what they had just seen was the Mothman.

Even though it happened 20 years ago, Misty and Brooke still vividly recall that frightful night when the Mothman stalked them.

Around this same time, it is quite possible that Misty's dad saw the same creature.

The following is her dad's account:

A hollow in the Cloverlick area of Harlan County is named "Refrigerator Hollow." It got this nickname because it seems much cooler there than elsewhere. This is probably because of the ice-cold water that flows from a stream off Black Mountain and winds down through the hollow. This area is close in proximity to Slope Hollow.

One day, Misty's dad decided to go hunting in Refrigerator Hollow. He was an experienced hunter who enjoyed being out in the woods. On this day, however, he encountered something he had never seen before. Up ahead of him, he saw a huge figure. It was standing upright, so he assumed it was a fellow hunter.

As he approached the figure, he stopped dead in his tracks. This tall, slim figure was not human – it appeared to be a bird. He stared at it intensely, trying to identify what was before him. It was extremely tall with enormous wings.

Hearing someone approaching, the colossal creature turned its head. Shockingly, it had a human face. Misty's dad began running wildly through the woods. The giant bird with a human face did not seem to follow or chase him.

When he arrived home, he was noticeably shaken. This concerned his family because they had rarely seen him like this. He told them about his terrifying experience but refused to discuss it afterward. Misty and her dad both encountered the giant birdlike creature at different times.

Misty and her dad are not alone; there have been several accounts of giant owls or birdlike creatures spotted in Harlan County near or on Black Mountain.

The following was contributed by John Gilliam and McKensi Johnson.

The Phantom of Cumberland Highschool

John is in the mental health profession and has always believed that the paranormal could be explained by mental health issues or the mind playing tricks. That is until he began dating McKensi, whose family are firm believers in the supernatural.

One night in 2017, John, McKensi, and her brother were taking a late-night drive through Cumberland when the topic of ghosts came up. John told them his firm stance of disbelief, and they told him they could show him a ghost right then.

They tell him to drive to the abandoned Cumberland High School building. Once there, they told John to look at the third window on the left of the third floor in the original part of the building. According to McKensi and her brother, the constant paranormal activity could be seen in that window nearly all the time.

Upon arrival at the school, McKensi and her brother immediately began seeing what they claimed was a ghost in the window. When John looked up at the specified window, he couldn't see anything. Disappointed, he blamed the other two for playing a trick on him. He wanted to see something paranormal and disprove his theory.

John decided to get his cousin, Cody, one of his most trusted friends. If Cody could see something in the window, then John would believe everyone except himself could see the ghost.

John drove the short distance to Cody's house and returned to the school. This time, his car hadn't even stopped when he and Cody clearly saw a figure moving back and forth in the window.

At this point, they get out their cell phones and begin videotaping this phenomenon. There are several good tapes of something veering back and forth on the school's third floor.

McKensi has had many experiences at the old Cumberland High School building since 2015. She and her friends liked driving around and would park at the high school building to hang out and talk. One night, they noticed the white figure in the window. They watched it for hours and began playing with it. They would move, and the white figure would follow them. If they drove forward, it would move in the same direction. Once, they tried to play a trick on it and threw their car in reverse, and the figure suddenly stopped abruptly and returned to where they were. This is an intelligent being.

McKensi began taking different friends to see the phantom in the window. She took several photographs and watched it so much that she eventually tired of it. She hadn't thought much of it in years until she wanted to prove to John that ghosts were real.

After John saw the phantom, both he and McKensi became fascinated with it and got permission from the Cumberland Police Department to go into the building and see if they could have a close encounter with it or at least find out what this thing was.

In April 2017, they went inside the building at midday. It was a warm, sunny day, and they snapped several pictures as they walked around the hallways and classrooms. They didn't realize they had captured anything until after they had left, and upon inspecting the photos, they noticed a figure in one of them. They decided to go back again that night.

Although the building seemed peaceful in the daytime, nighttime was a different story. They were shocked by a loud bang when they entered through the cafeteria door. They continued through the school and toward the gymnasium when a high-pitched voice called, "Yoohoo!' As the voice carried through the hallway, a cold breeze blew by. This was enough to panic them, so they quickly exited. As they headed out the door, the loud bang sounded again, just as it did when they entered. Luckily, they were videotaping when they heard the voice call out and recorded it.

John and McKensi began going to the school building nearly every night, trying to see and hear more paranormal activity. John was becoming obsessed with trying to debunk and rationalize what he was seeing. One night, they returned with a friend who had done some paranormal investigating and owned various equipment.

They could hear something huge jumping up and down on the floor above them as soon as they entered the building. It had to be something of substantial size to create the sound it was making. If that were not unnerving enough, the smell of rotting meant lofted all around them. A wind began blowing, and a breathy, faint voice said, "Go."

Once, John was on the third floor exploring when he decided to go into a classroom. A freezing cold wind hit him in the face when he opened the door. An intense pain went up his arm, and he could feel something tugging at it. He quickly ran out of the room and down the stairs.

After they heard the command, "Go," they never saw the figure in the third-floor window again. It was as if their presence caused it to move on. The old school is boarded up now and falling into disrepair. All John and McKensi have of the Cumberland High School phantom are photographs, videotapes, and an occasional nightmare.

Cumberland High School building,

Cumberland, Kentucky

McHenry Fields

In 1973, Jerry was 18 years old and excited about getting a good job with the forestry department, marking property lines and reclaiming land. A native of Lynch, Kentucky, Jerry often worked on or around Black Mountain. On this particular day, he was working near McHenry Fields on Black Mountain toward Eolia, which is in Letcher County.

Jerry's boss and another coworker weren't as good at maneuvering the mountain as Jerry, so they drove to a hollow, let him out, and planned to pick him up on the Eolia side of the tract of land. The property line Jerry was marking was far too rough for the four-wheel drive truck that they were in. His boss gave him red paint for marking trees and a machete to get through high weeds and brush. Jerry was told to follow the hollow to the top of Black Mountain, where he would come out at McHenry Fields, an old settlement with only remnants of farmhouses and barns remaining.

Jerry set out toward McHenry Fields as his boss told him to watch for copperheads. It was a warm spring day, and the snakes would be sunning themselves on rocks and dirt path. As he walked through the hollow, he began to see old rock foundations where houses once stood and discarded belongings from days gone by. He found it all very interesting.

After a while, Jerry came to a clearing, and the dirt path became large enough for a vehicle. He saw more rock foundations with crocuses and Easter lilies blooming in flower gardens of long ago. He had been instructed to walk toward the right because that was where the truck would meet him and pick him back up. Jerry was amazed at how many houses had been there at one time. He never realized how large the settlement at McHenry Fields had been. He was enjoying the beautiful morning and looking at the old settlement.

Jerry passed by ancient orchards and crumbling rock walls. As he continued, he came upon an old man sitting on the rock wall. The old man was wearing bibbed overalls and a button-down shirt. Jerry greeted him, and they politely commented on the beautiful morning and good weather. The old man said, "Mornings like this, I love to come out here and sit on this rock wall and enjoy the day. I think this is one of the most beautiful places in the world." Jerry told him about what he was doing and that he was meeting his boss and coworker on the other side of the field. The old man told him he hadn't seen a vehicle up there yet. After talking for a few more minutes, Jerry told the old man that the truck should surely be up there, so he needed to meet them. They said goodbye, and the old man jokingly told him not to work too hard.

Jerry headed on the dirt road for another mile before seeing his boss's truck. It was further than he had thought it would be. As he got in the truck, he asked the two other men if they had seen another vehicle on the road. They said that they were the only vehicle on that road. Jerry told him that he took longer than he should have because he stopped and talked to an old man. On the walk to the truck, he began to wonder how the man got there and where his truck was. He was far too old to walk from Eolia, or anywhere for that matter. He was a very elderly man.

As they rode off the mountain, Jerry realized there was no reasonable explanation for the old man's presence at the McHenry Fields. As he recalled his conversation with him, he recalled that the old man was wearing clothing that was worn many years ago – not in the 1970s. The old man appeared to be 90 or 100 years old. Only then did he realize he was talking to one of the residents who settled in that area decades ago? Jerry had been talking to the ghost of an old settler who, even after death, loved McHenry Fields so much that he decided to stay for all eternity.

The Ghost of the Doctor's Office

In downtown Harlan, there is a building that used to be a doctor's office. The office has long closed and is now used for other purposes. Susan started working there in the late 1980s as a receptionist and did so for 15 years.

As soon as Susan started working there, she began hearing strange sounds. The sounds would start in the front of the office in the morning and end in the back of the building in the evening. It began with jingling keys and heavy footsteps walking across the floor when no one was there. Susan would check and see if someone had entered the waiting room, but they had yet to. She would check on the doctor and nurses, and they would all be busy with paperwork, not making a sound.

Once, all three employees were sitting in the same office when they heard the busy shuffling of papers. Thinking maybe the doctor had returned, Susan checked, and no one else was there. She even checked the back door, and it was locked.

Most times, the activity started during the lunch break. Water would turn on, and the copy machine would start by itself as if something didn't like them taking their break. Many items would fall off tables or sinks without anyone being nearby. Susan and her co-workers finally got tired of the disruptions and would shout loudly at it, telling it to leave them alone.

One day, a supervisor came in for a staff meeting. Susan closed the office and locked the door when it was meeting time. Even though the door was locked, the sound of it opening and closing loudly echoed through the building. The supervisor asked Susan to see who it was, and she replied that she had locked the door and no one could enter. Sure enough, when they checked, the door had been securely locked.

Through the years, Susan and the office staff got used to their ghostly activity and often ignored it. They never felt afraid or threatened by it. Susan thinks the ghost was an employee of the past continuing their duties as they had when they were alive.

This occurrence happened in Benham, Kentucky, in the 1920s.

The Hairy Man of Benham, Kentucky

A man named Andrew, who lived up a hollow in Benham, awoke to a dreadful discovery. He went out to feed his dogs, and to his shock, they had all been killed and stacked up on top of one another. These dogs were secured in a lot, somewhat near his home. It just didn't make sense that something broke into the lot, killed the dogs, and went to the trouble of stacking them by twos. Stranger still, there were no wounds on the animals, and the only possible cause of death Andrew could determine was that something broke their necks.

Although upset by losing all four of his dogs in a horrific way, Andrew had to go to work. He planned on burying the dogs after he got back home. His brother, Christopher, worked at the same coal mine, so Andrew told him about the bizarre killing that had taken place. After hearing about it, Christopher told Andrew that whatever killed the dogs was probably planning to carry them off and ran away when it saw Andrew coming.

Christopher told Andrew that he believed that whatever killed his dogs would come back for them that night. The brothers began devising a light they could set at the dog lot and turn on when they heard something coming. They created this with a carbide mining light and a long cord with a switch at the end.

Andrew and Christopher set up their light and sat quietly in the dark near the dog lot with their shotguns. Sure enough, at about 10:30 p.m., they heard something walking through the woods toward the lot. They quietly listened, and when they heard it getting into the dog lot, they quickly switched on the light.

To their terror, there, in the glow of the carbide light, was a huge hairy apelike man standing around eight feet tall. The vast creature seemed shocked and quickly turned and ran back into the woods.

The brothers sat frozen in fear, and although Andrew planned on shooting whatever had killed his dogs, he could not move a muscle after seeing this large, hairy man. There was no doubt that the creature had killed his dogs the night before and come back for them. Andrew and Christopher had never seen anything like it, and the sight was so shocking that they stared in disbelief.

Andrew later got more dogs but moved his dog lot very close to the house, lit it up with lanterns, and kept a loaded gun near his bed just in case the giant hairy creature tried to make a second attempt at killing his dogs.

This story was contributed by Cody Williamson.

The House Near Blair Lake

There used to be a beautiful white two-story house near Blair Lake in the Cumberland area leading to Letcher County. The house burned down years ago, but many say it had a tragic past. At one point in time, a mother struggled to deal with her small child. In desperation and exhaustion, the young woman pushed her child, and it fell into the fire in the fireplace, killing it. Years passed, and the incident was forgotten.

Years later, some young people played with an Ouija board in the house and began giving dates and names. They learned from their grandmother that it had given them the name and death date of the child killed in the house.

Many people had strange experiences in the house, and one time, every light and ceiling fan in the entire house came on at once, sending the occupants running out the door.

Finally, the old house burned down, and although it was blamed on electrical issues, many claim it was the child who had died there, eventually destroying the house like it had perished there years before.

The Swimmer at Martins Fork Lake

Martins Fork Lake in the Smith area of Harlan County was developed in the 1970s. Before the lake was created, the land had rolling hillsides, farms, and homesteads. It is now a recreational area with swimming, fishing, picnicking, and hiking. Many locals and tourists enjoy visiting this beautiful body of water surrounded by green mountains. It is a picturesque sight, indeed.

Over the years, there have been tales of water creatures in the world's lakes and oceans. What appears to be giant serpents inhabit the waters, occasionally giving onlookers a brief glimpse. Martins Fork Lake does not have a creature like this lurking in its depth, but there does seem to be something inhuman swimming through the water.

On several occasions, visitors to the lake claim to see something swimming in the water. The swimmer never seems to reach the bank; once it goes under, it never returns. Witnesses say something resembling a human swims near the buoys and safety ropes. It never reaches the bank and appears too far out in the water to be an average swimmer. Onlookers begin watching the swimmer out of concern and are bewildered when it swims off through the water or goes back under. There is never a sign of a struggle or potential drowning. The swimmer seems calm and collected as they make their way through the water.

One eyewitness was at the lake with her boyfriend in September 2020. The couple enjoyed a warm, late-summer evening, taking one last swim before autumn settled in. As they sat drying off at the beach, something popped out of the water near the buoys. Neither had seen anyone else come to the beach to swim. The figure seemed to stand up in the water, which was impossible due to its depth. It was tall and slim, with the entirety of its chest and torso exposed for a brief moment. It then immersed itself underwater and never appeared again. The couple intently watched for it to reappear, but it never did.

People who see this phenomenon always assume it is a swimmer in trouble. Still, after investigating, they determined that no swimmers could be in the water due to weather conditions or other circumstances, like a completely deserted beach or parking area. This swimmer pops up randomly and never shows signs of being in trouble.

It is often speculated as to who or what this phantom swimmer is. Many say that it is the apparition of one of the many unfortunate drowning victims of the lake. Martins Fork Lake has had numerous drownings over the years. Others say it is the former residents of the farms and houses that stood where the lake is now. Old farmers checking on their fields and gardens, utterly unaware that a large body of water now exists where they lived and worked for many years. No one will probably ever know the exact reason for the sightings of the ghostly swimmer, but all who see it say that there is something otherworldly and surreal about it.

Martins Fork Lake

Buoys at the Martins Fork Lake Beach

The House of Spirits

In 1985, Belinda Taylor lived in the house she currently does at Wallins Creek. During this time, she began hearing a baby crying in the house. Because there were no babies there, she began trying to find the source of the sound to explain it. Strangely, whenever she would go to the bedroom where it was coming from, the crying would stop as she touched the doorknob. The sound of the crying baby would not happen for a long time and then suddenly start back up again.

One night, Belinda was awakened by the sound of the crying. She got up and went toward the bedroom it was coming from. As usual, when she touched the doorknob, it stopped. She went into the room and sat down on the bed. She began trying to console the baby and told it everything would be fine. The baby stopped crying, and it never happened again.

Later, Belinda learned many years ago that a woman who was mentally ill lived in the home across the street. She kidnapped a neighborhood baby, thinking it was hers. When she realized it was not and people were searching for the baby, she took it to the outhouse and threw it in the toilet, killing it. Belinda believes that the infant who died across the street is the source of the crying in her home.

The sound of the crying baby stopped, but other activity in the home continued. Belinda's daughter often saw a man down the hall and screamed in terror. She said the man was dressed in brown and looked to be in his mid-fifties. Belinda discovered that the man who previously lived there had been found dead in the home. His description resembled the man her daughter often saw in the hallway. Her daughter was so terrified of the man that Belinda begged him to stop scaring her child. Her daughter never saw it after that.

In May of 2021, Belinda awoke one night to the sound of a woman laughing and talking. Assuming someone was outside her house, she shouted, telling them to please leave and that they were trespassing. The sounds stopped, but five minutes later, the sound of heavy footsteps running down the hall began, with the sound of laughing all the while. Belinda ran out into the hallway, and nothing was there.

Belinda's house has had many paranormal events, but she continues to live there and lets the spirits know when they get too disruptive.

The Clown

In 1965, when Nora was about six years old, she and her family lived in Cumberland in an older house with wood floors. One day, while she was in the living room, a "clown" came out from a crack in the wood floor. He had no hair, pale skin, and wore white clothes. He had exaggerated features and simply walked around the house. Being so young, Nora didn't exactly understand what was going on. This was the first time she saw him, and she recalls him staying in the house awhile but doesn't remember him leaving.

The clown continued to come out of the crack in the floor for years after that. He always came out during the daytime. As she got older, Nora became so disturbed by this clown that her mother took her to a psychiatrist in Harlan. No one else in her family saw the clown, so they assumed she had mental issues. He never made a sound but always smiled eerily at her. He didn't come out very often, but when he did, Nora was terrified. She lived in constant dread of this bizarre entity.

Years passed, and one night, when Nora was around 13 years old, she heard a primal screeching scream and the sound of someone beating on metal. She instantly knew it was the clown. He was angry because he could no longer enter her home. Seeing the clown was very upsetting to her, but the sound it made was by far the most disturbing thing it ever did. It was a horrific sound that made her tremble with fear.

Now, Nora says that the clown somehow manifested through the energy of a child. She had gone through puberty, and he could no longer use her as a conduit. Whatever this thing was, it needed a child, and once she was not a child anymore, it became powerless.

The clown never returned, and Nora still does not know exactly what it was. Although it never threatened her, its presence was a returning horror that affected her childhood greatly. Nora's family no longer lives in the house, but it is still standing and has other tenants. She often wonders if any of the children have had to endure the presence of the clown that comes out of the crack in the wood floor.

Headless Annie

One of the most legendary tales in Harlan County is that of Headless Annie. The story originated in the 1930s and seems to have sprung up during the violence associated with the unionizing of the coal mines. The most common tale of Headless Annie is that she was the young daughter of a coal miner who was beheaded in front of her family by thugs hired by the coal company. According to the legend, the entire family was murdered by the hired assassins.

The legend states that Headless Annie roams the night looking for her head. She is most seen on the side of the road in Lynch, Kentucky, and up to the peak of Black Mountain. Because she seems to be a roadside apparition, there is a secondary tale of a woman being beheaded in a car accident. Both accounts seem to be undocumented, and there has never been a surname or identity found for young Annie.

Firsthand accounts of encountering Headless Annie are few and far between. After years of research, we finally discovered a very recent sighting of the headless ghost – during the pandemic of 2020. A family returning from a drive to Wise County, Virginia, saw her near the Lynch Country Club. They claim a headless young girl was standing by the road in what seemed to be a schoolgirl's dress with buttons and puffed sleeves.

After much research, we now have a much earlier encounter with the ghost. Unfortunately, this is not a firsthand experience but a secondhand one passed down from father to son. Gregory says his father told him this tale until he passed away in 2009.

Gregory's father, Charles, was born in 1939 in Lynch, Kentucky, and lived there until he joined the Army in the mid-1960s. His experience happened in the early fall of 1963, just before his 24th birthday. He told his story to his children, grandchildren, and anyone else who would listen. He was steadfast that this was a true story and the most terrifying thing he'd ever seen.

In September of 1963, Charles was turning 24, getting married to his sweetheart, Carol, and planning on joining the Army in early 1964. He felt that the carefree days of youth were coming to an end, so he wanted one last get-together with his high school buddies. On a warm Saturday night in late September, the four young men went to a local high school football game, sat in the parking lot afterward, and drank beer. It was just like old times.

At some point, when the beer was taking effect, they decided it would be fun to go to the foot of Black Mountain, where the picnic tables were. It was a short drive, and soon, they were lying on top of the tables, looking at the stars and drinking more beer.

By midnight, they all felt quite drunk and decided it was time to go home. Although it was fun pretending to be a teenager again, in reality, they had jobs, and a couple of them were married. They all loaded up in the big 1956 Chevy and headed toward home. Charles was driving, and as they made their way toward Lynch, something from the side of the road seemed to fall out into the middle of the road. Quickly, Charles swerved and ended up in a ditch.

The other three young men howled with laughter and called Charles a drunk. Although he had been drinking, he was no longer feeling the influence. Something had just thrown itself into the road in front of the car, which had a very sobering effect on him. He told them what he had seen, and as expected, the taunting and laughter continued.

The three young men got out to push the car back on the highway while Charles stayed in the car to steer it. He watched the men in his rearview mirror acting foolishly while pushing with all their might. To his relief, he felt the big Chevy finally inch its way back to the road. He continued to watch his friends when something behind them caught his eye. It seemed to be a young girl in a dress slowly walking toward the car.

Charles couldn't believe his eyes as the girl in the dress got closer. It looked as if she didn't have a head or a face. He saw remnants of long hair, but other than that, the collar of her dress was the next thing visible. Charles quickly turned to get a better look, and she was as plain as day, with the rear-view lights turning her all aglow.

Charles began yelling for his friends to get in the car. He was so panic-stricken that they didn't question him. They ran to the car, jumped in, and Charles pushed the gas as far as it would go. Within minutes, they were close to home. Charles didn't say much as he let two of his friends out. Charles told him what he had seen when it was just him and his best friend, Kenneth. Kenneth begged Charles to go back and see if it was still there, but he would not. He said that was a sight he never wanted to see again.

Within a year, Charles moved away from Lynch and never moved back. He lived most of his life in Indiana. Although time passed and things changed, he never forgot the night he saw the infamous Headless Annie of Lynch, Kentucky. When he told about the night, he always said that the thing that threw itself into the road was also related to the ghost, if not the ghost herself. He couldn't swear to it, but he thought it was the dress he saw falling into the road, causing him to swerve.

Charles' family says that he gave that night much thought, and it was something he talked about frequently. He visited Lynch once every year or so and, at night, would drive up to Black Mountain and slowly drive back down as if searching for the apparition. Although he claimed he didn't want to see her again, something kept drawing him back to Headless Annie.

The Other Side of Black Mountain

Harlan Countians tend to forget that Black Mountain is shared with Wise County, Virginia, and parts of Lee County. This Virginia area has its share of unusual tales and accounts of strange happenings on and around Black Mountain. This area contains a rich history, much of it deep with mystery and lore. A treasure trove of stories has been told for generations of mysterious creatures and phenomena unexplained in and around the communities of Big Stone Gap and Appalachia, Virginia. The following are a few of my favorites.

The Hitchhiking Girl

When David Hartford was a young man, he liked to run around with his friends, Billy and Bobby. Billy had a souped-up '69 Ford, and they were coming home from a bowling alley in Virginia. All three were sitting in the front seat drinking beer as they approached Inman, Virginia, the last community before you begin the trek up and over Black Mountain to Lynch.

As they drove along through Inman, they came upon a beautiful young woman hitchhiking. Because she was so attractive, Billy didn't hesitate to stop and pick her up. David assumed she must be going to a party somewhere because she was all dressed in a pretty white dress.

The girl got in the backseat without saying a word. Billy kept talking to the girl, but she didn't respond. As they approached the last house in Inman, Billy asked her if she wanted out there or if she was going to Lynch. He kept looking in the rear-view mirror at her but then suddenly threw on his brakes.

David and Bobby looked over at him, wondering what he was doing. Billy said, "You aren't going to believe this, but she is gone." David and Bobby turned quickly to the backseat, and it was empty. No one was there, and they never saw her again. They had never stopped the car, and it is still a mystery as to what got in the backseat with them that night.

Booger Holler

In 1960, a young man from Appalachia, Virginia, had a terrifying experience. He and his family lived up a hollow all to themselves. Their grandparents had built their house and farm in the late 1800s, and the only way to get there was by foot. The old farmhouse was about three miles up the hollow.

Until the young man reached his teens, his father used to walk him down the footpath to the highway to catch the school bus, then meet him in the afternoon to walk with him back home. When he started high school, his parents felt he was old enough to do it alone. He would leave his house before daylight and get home after dark during the colder months.

In November of 1960, the young man headed out on a Tuesday morning as he always did. When he was in the most secluded area, about a mile and a half into his trek, he began to hear something that seemed to be following him. He always carried his flashlight and scanned the wood line with it. He didn't see anything, and he continued on his way.

It wasn't long before he could hear dry twigs and leaves crackling in the woods. It was a cool, crisp morning, and all was unusually still. Not a sound could be heard except the peculiar sounds of something moving in the forest. The young man was accustomed to hunting and being in the wilderness, so when small tree limbs began breaking, he knew this was an animal of great size. Maybe a bear had wandered in from North Carolina. He moved quickly, and soon, he was at the bus stop.

He didn't forget about the unusual sounds that day, so as soon as he got off the bus that afternoon, he quickly headed toward home, trying to get there before dark. Usually, he would stand around with his friends and chat before heading up the hollow. Today was different; he desperately wanted to be home by sundown.

Unfortunately, dusk came too soon, and as he went deeper and deeper into the hollow, the sun dropped down behind the mountain, and nightfall approached. He got out his flashlight and walked as fast as he could.

He hadn't gone far before hearing the leaves crackling again. This time, he didn't wait around and listen. He broke into a run, and to his horror, whatever was following him ran steadily after him with big footsteps pounding the ground. The young man ran as fast as he ever had in his life, and the thundering steps behind him became distant. He was outrunning it for now, but probably not for long. He couldn't run at that speed on the way home, so he made a crucial decision. As soon as he ran around a steep curve out of sight, he jumped over the bank and into a pile of leaves. He quickly covered himself up and lay there dead still.

Soon, he heard the creature approach the path above him. He dared not move a muscle. Some of the leaves fell away from his eyes, and in the moonlight, he could see a massive beast standing on the path, looking side to side for him. It was everything he could do not to scream and run, but his life depended on his silence.

The huge creature looked like an ape and was covered with matted hair. It had a huge head and large dangling arms. As a breeze blew his way, he could smell a musky, pungent odor he had never smelled before. He continued to hide in the leaves with beads of perspiration popping out on his forehead. The beast began making a growling sound, unlike anything he had ever heard. Then, it roared as if it were angry that the boy had escaped.

Finally, the creature turned and ran back down the hollow toward the highway. The young man lay there for about 20 minutes more before making a move. When he felt it was safe, he bolted out of the leaves and sprinted toward home. Soon, he began to feel safer and stopped taking a few deep breaths before continuing. As soon as he stopped, he heard the terrifying sound of the thunderous steps on the path behind him. It was back! He ran as fast as he could in sheer panic.

Luckily, he saw his house in the distance. When he got close enough, he began yelling for his father. The porch light came on, and his father came out. The boy ran up on the porch and pushed his father back into the house, locking the door behind them.

Soon, the hunting dogs emerged from under the porch, barking wildly at the beast. It had followed him all the way to the porch steps. Above the dogs' barks, they could hear the growling and roaring of the enormous creature. Finally, after a fierce fight, all was quiet, and the boy told his parents what had happened. He and his father stayed up all night with their shotguns, watching for the beast.

The following day, all the dogs lay dead in the yard. The creature had literally ripped them apart. The young man's father notified the sheriff of what had happened. The police searched the entire area but found nothing except a tuft of reddish-brown hair caught in the barn fence. They sent the hair to Richmond, Virginia, for identification, and the results came back as "unknown origin."

After that, the young man and his parents moved away from their family farm and into the town of Appalachia. They could never feel safe again in the hollow, and he could never walk to the bus and back home with any peace of mind. The terrifying creature interrupted their simple way of living and caused them to give up a home they dearly loved.

The old homeplace stood in ruins until it finally fell to the ground about 20 years ago. Few venture up to where the farmhouse and barn once stood. Only hunters and a few naïve hikers travel the footpath now. To the locals, it is now called Booger Holler, named after the creature, that ran a family out of there, never to return.

The Winged Dog

Elijah was born in the early 1900s in Wise County, Virginia. After he had raised his family, he and his wife lived alone in a large farmhouse near the town of Appalachia at the foot of Big Black Mountain. The old two-story white house did not have indoor plumbing in the 1940s. It still had an outhouse set a good distance from the house. They lived the old way, and that is the way they liked it.

In the summer of 1946, Elijah heard something creeping across the front porch. The porch extended the entire length of the house, and it seemed that whatever it was would go from one side of it to the other. Sometimes, it sounded like something walking around the house, and a few times, Elijah swore it sounded like something trying to take the screens off the windows. During the summer, the screens were the only protection from the outside. Windows were open all summer long. Elijah kept a pistol by the bed, and every time he heard it, he would get his gun and look outside but never saw anything. He asked his wife, Eva, if she had heard it, but she hadn't.

One night, after Elijah had gotten the wood in for the cookstove for breakfast in the morning, he decided to turn in. It was about 10:30 PM, which was rather late for country people. He would make one more trip to the outhouse before going to bed. He grabbed his pistol and lantern and headed outside.

The moon was out, but it was a partly cloudy night sky, so visibility was still low. As Elijah walked the little footpath to the outhouse, he began hearing something in the high weeds beside him. It sounded like something trying to be very quiet following him. As quiet as it tried to be, he could still hear dry weeds cracking under the weight of something. The steps were slow and steady. Elijah could tell it was something big and assumed it was a fox or coyote. Whatever it was, slowly and steadily followed Elijah to the outhouse. He was beginning to get nervous.

He came out of the outhouse and stood for a few minutes to see if he could hear it anymore. Hopefully, whatever it was had moved on. Everything was quiet, and Elijah felt relieved, but as soon as he started back to the house, it began following him again as if it had been waiting on him. He then began fearing it might be a bear stalking him, so he picked up his pace and started listening very carefully.

He was walking so fast that his lantern began casting strange shadows, making him more uncomfortable than ever. The house never seemed so far away; he held his pistol tight and walked quickly. Elijah was breathing heavily, for he knew animals did not stalk humans – they typically try to avoid them. Something was not right.

Elijah broke into a run, and when he did, something flew out of the weeds directly at him. He could feel the breeze as it passed by his face. The flapping of its wings made a loud, roaring sound. This was much bigger than an owl or any bird that lived in the area, and Elijah felt sheer terror. Before he could run again, he heard something coming up behind him. He whirled around and couldn't believe his eyes. There, in the middle of the road, was a black dog with wings.

Elijah tried to run, but as soon as he moved, it spread its enormous wings out from its body. Its wingspan was about eight feet long. It had long fangs and every time Elijah turned to run, it would growl deep and guttural. Although he was trembling, he knew his only hope was his pistol. He wasn't sure if he could even shoot it, but he had to try. He pointed the gun at the dog and fired every bullet he had into the dog. As soon as shots made contact, the dog exploded into white dust. Elijah ran through the falling white powder and into his house. He never saw anything like that again, but through the years, he told anyone who would listen about the night he encountered the winged dog.

The Stranger and His Dog

Many years ago, there was a hollow between Appalachia and Big Stone Gap, Virginia, home to the Short family. There were a few small farmhouses set a mile or so apart in this hollow, and everyone who lived there was related or knew each other well.

Around 1910, Jewel and her family lived in one of these farmhouses in Short Hollow. Her grandparents had one of the first houses ever built there. Grandpa Short had raised his family and watched his grandchildren thrive there. Jewel lived in a small white house near the road, as many were in those days. Built before automobiles, there was no need for a home to be far away from the road. It was more convenient, and noise or dust wasn't an issue. Travelers often walked or rode horses, and cars were a rare luxury reserved for townspeople.

Jewel would sit in front of the living room window most summer afternoons and embroider or sew. She enjoyed the breeze and loved the view of the meadow with all the daisies in bloom. One day, she noticed a man walking down the hollow with his dog. He was one of the tallest men she'd ever seen, dressed all in black. He walked his dog on a leash, and it had pointed ears and looked rather ferocious. It was a strange sight, especially since everyone in the hollow knew each other. Strangers never ventured into the hollow, and Jewel wondered who he was visiting.

A few weeks later, Jewel was helping her mother in the garden near the roadside. Her mother was on one side, and she was on the other. She was on her knees picking peppers and putting them in her apron when she heard someone walking up the road. It was the stranger and his dog again. Jewel quickly put her head down and busied herself, fearing the man would catch her staring at him. He was even taller than she remembered and was an odd sight, indeed. His dog stayed close to him as he did the first time she saw them.

Jewel kept her head low as they passed but got a good look at the man this time. His skin was dark, and his eyes were jet-black and set far apart. He had an unusually wide forehead that gave him a very bizarre appearance. As the man passed, he stared straight at her, scaring her so badly she spilled the peppers everywhere. The stranger and his dog walked up the hollow without saying a word.

A few nights later, Jewel was in bed but unable to sleep. She tossed and turned and then finally began to feel comfortable and sleepy. She began hearing two men talking and strained her ears to see what they were saying. She couldn't make out any words but heard them conversing outside her window. She lay there for about five minutes listening before she crept out of bed to see who it was. She slowly tiptoed to the window, and there, by the edge of the road, was the stranger and his dog. She scanned the area for the other man involved in the conversation but saw no one. Until she approached the window, she had heard an entire two-part conversation with two distinct male voices. The stranger said something to the dog and began walking out of the hollow. Jewel watched them until they went out of sight.

She got back into bed but once again couldn't sleep. She found it disturbing that they were right outside the house at that time of night. She found it very bizarre that there weren't two men outside, just the stranger and his dog. Where had the other man gone?

Other people in the hollow were talking about the stranger and his dog. Jewel and her family weren't the only ones who saw them. Most residents of Short Hollow had seen them, and no one seemed to know who they were. People were getting concerned about them and their reason for being there. Perhaps they were up to no good. They were most definitely not visitors or company. Everyone would keep a close eye on them until they left for good.

A couple of weeks passed, and as Jewel was getting ready for bed one night, a feeling of dread came over her. Despite her apprehension, she turned off the oil light on her nightstand and got in bed. She soon fell into a deep sleep. Sometime in the middle of the night, she was awakened by a shuffling sound in her room. She assumed it was her cat coming to get in bed with her as it often did. She had just fallen back asleep when she felt something crawl into bed with her. Her eyes flew open, and the stranger's dog was at the foot of the bed making its way toward her.

The huge dog's eyes stared at her as if trying to put her in a trance. Jewel was finding it hard to breathe and felt like a weight was resting on her chest. The dog seemed shocked she was awake and lay there, staring at her and breathing heavily. Jewel could finally move, so she jumped up, grabbed the poker from the fireplace, and struck the dog in the head, making a gash above its eye. With blood pouring down its face, the dog jumped up and ran out the kitchen screen door. As the dog was running out, Jewel's father was running in to see what was wrong.

Because of the chaos the night before, the entire family got up early that morning. Jewel's father said he would find the stranger to tell him about his dog coming into the house. Jewel saw the stranger and his dog coming up the road about that time. The stranger turned to look at her and smiled an ominous smile. He removed his top hat, put one arm across his waist, and gave her a bow. She got a good look at his forehead as he bowed to her. There was a gash above his eye. She then looked at the dog – it didn't have a wound at all. With that, the stranger and the dog walked out of the holler, never to be seen again.

Made in United States
Troutdale, OR
04/12/2024

19132015R00126